THE MONEY GUN

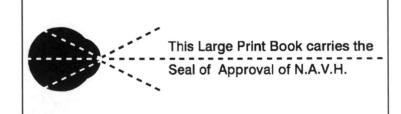

This Large Print Book carries the
Seal of Approval of N.A.V.H.

THE MONEY GUN

ROBERT J. RANDISI

WHEELER PUBLISHING
A part of Gale, Cengage Learning

GALE
CENGAGE Learning

Detroit • New York • San Francisco • New Haven, Conn • Waterville, Maine • London

GALE
CENGAGE Learning™

LIBRARY OF CONGRESS CATALOGING-IN-PUBLICATION DATA

Randisi, Robert J.
   The money gun / by Robert J. Randisi.
     p. cm.
   ISBN-13: 978-1-59722-739-1 (softcover : alk. paper)
   ISBN-10: 1-59722-739-0 (softcover : alk. paper)
   1. Large type books. I. Title.
  PS3568.A53M66 2008
  813'.54—dc22   2008002705

Published in 2008 by arrangement with Leisure Books, a division of Dorchester Publishing Co., Inc.

THE MONEY GUN

CHAPTER 1

Center, Montana, 1898

Faulkner rode into Center, Montana, on an eight-year-old bay mare that had seen better days. He figured once he completed his business there he'd see about buying a new horse. He bought and used horses the way he did his saddle, saddlebags and bedroll. They were all things he needed, but the need was not specific to any one item. A horse was a horse, and to illustrate that fact, he never named his mounts. His friend Henry Tall Fellow had once advised him never to name something you might one day have to eat.

Center was no different from any of the thousands of towns Faulkner had been to over the past twenty-two years. Not large, not small, it was not near a mine or adjacent to rich grazing land. It did not have the growth potential that many of the boom towns had. It was stuck right where it was in its development, and while it would probably never grow any larger, there was a chance that it would begin to die when people realized that and chose to leave.

The buildings that lined Main Street were worn and faded. Even where some folks had slapped on a fresh coat of paint in an attempt to hide or cover the despair, it bled through.

Faulkner found his way to a livery stable, which, in keeping with the tone of the town, looked as if a stiff wind would blow it over. He was going to need to stay over a night, though, to complete the task that had brought him there, and the condition of the place did not alarm him enough to send him looking for something better. He very much doubted there was something better.

He dismounted in front of the livery and walked the animal inside. A stringy fellow, who could have been anywhere from fifty to eighty, walked toward him, carrying a bale of hay.

"You wanna leave your horse?" the man asked.

"Just overnight," Faulkner said. "I should be out of here by morning."

"Don't know why you'd wanna be here in the first place," the man muttered. He tossed the hay into a stall and wiped his hands on his backside as he came closer and eyed the mare.

"Don't look like such a much," he said.

"She ain't," Faulkner said. "Fact is, my intention was to buy a new horse, but this town doesn't fill me with much confidence to that end."

"Town don't matter," the livery man said. "Fact is, I got me some good stock out back you can look at if you've a mind to."

"Good stock? You sure?"

"I been at this a long time, friend," the man said. "I know good horseflesh when I see it. This ain't it. Oh, she mighta been once, but she's plumb wore out, and she shouldn't be. What is she, eight?"

"Yep."

"She's been rid hard in her life," the man said. "That from you?"

"Last couple of years," Faulkner admitted.

"You're hard on a horse."

"Can't deny it."

The man took off his hat, scratched the full head of gray hair he still owned, then replaced the worn hat.

"Maybe I shouldn't sell you a horse, but fact is I can't be choosy. You wanna look at 'em, ya can."

"In the morning," Faulkner said. "What's

your name?"

"Thatcher."

Faulkner handed the stable man the mare's reins. Thatcher eyed the saddle with some distaste.

"Looks like you might be needin' a new saddle soon, too."

"That's true enough."

"Well, ya ain't gonna find that here, that's for sure. You want my advice? Stop off in Laramie. They got some good tack there for a man who needs it."

"I'll keep that in mind. Is there a good hotel in town?"

"No."

"A decent one?"

"Hell no. Tell ya whatcha do. Keep goin' here for a block past us and you'll see a two-story house that looks like it don't belong in this town 'cause it's too well cared for. That's the widow Gentry's rooming house. If you want a good night's sleep, that's the place to get it in Center."

"Well, I'm much obliged, Thatcher," Faulkner said. "Fact is, I think I'm going to be in need of a good night's sleep."

"You can't be in this town on business," the older man said.

"Oh, but I can."

"What kind of business would bring ya to

this godforsaken town?" Thatcher wondered.

"You'll know all about it by tomorrow," Faulkner told him, and he walked out. He turned in the direction recommended by the livery man.

Thatcher stared after Faulkner, noticed the man's well-cared-for weapon and the way he wore his gun belt. Also the way he stood in general, confident-like. He wasn't so much to look at, his clothes covered with trail dust, his face kind of plain, but there was an attitude about him. Thatcher had been around men like that a good long time, prided himself on being able to spot them.

This one didn't look the part at first glance, but Thatcher looked more than once and knew what he was looking at.

Shaking his head, he pulled the horse along and muttered to himself, "Money gun."

CHAPTER 2

Faulkner found his way to the widow Gentry's boardinghouse with no problem. Thatcher had described it perfectly. It was the only building in town that didn't reek of age and exhaustion. As he approached it he saw a small boy in front, maybe eight or nine years old, with blond hair. He was just standing, staring down at the ground. As Faulkner got closer, the boy didn't move a muscle.

"What are you looking at?" Faulkner asked.

"Nothin'," the boy said.

"You live here?"

The boy nodded.

"Your name Gentry?"

Now the boy looked up.

"Billy Gentry. How'd you know?"

"Lucky guess," Faulkner said. "I guess your grandma would be the widow Gentry who runs this house?"

"No, sir," Billy Gentry said, "that'd be my ma."

Faulkner had gotten the impression from talking to Thatcher that the widow Gentry was an older woman. Given the age of this boy, the lady was apparently a young widow.

"Would you know if she's got any rooms for rent?" he asked the boy.

"She's got plenty," the boy said. "She says this town ain't good for nothin' and that we may have to sell the house and move."

"That a fact?"

"Only she says a body'd have to be crazy to buy this house in this town. Mister?"

"Yeah?"

"Does that mean my pa was crazy? I mean, he bought this house in this town."

"Son, I'll bet when your pa bought this house this town was a mite more prosperous than it is now."

The boy screwed up his face.

"What's prosp-prospish?"

"It means the town probably had more people back then, and was in better shape."

"Oh. So he wasn't crazy?"

"I don't think so. Your ma home?"

"Yes, sir. Just go on up and knock on the door," Billy said. "She'll open it for ya."

"I'm much obliged for the information, Billy," Faulkner said. "You can go back to what you were doing."

"I wasn't doin' nothin' but starin'."

"And a fine job you were doing, too."

Faulkner walked past the boy and tousled his blond hair on the way. He mounted the steps and knocked on the front door.

"Yes?" The voice came from behind a screen, but moments later a woman appeared. She was tall, blond, built along angular lines, thirty but looking forty because she'd been working hard all her life. A handsome woman nevertheless.

"Mrs. Gentry?"

"Yes?"

"That fine young man out front told me you might have a room for rent," Faulkner said.

"Fine youn— oh, you mean Billy? Did he bother you?"

"Not at all," Faulkner said. "Truth be told he was very helpful, and real polite. You should be proud."

"I am, most of the time," she said, "but he is an eight-year-old boy."

"I understand."

"So you want a room? For how long?"

"Just overnight," he said. "I'll just be in town long enough to see to my business."

"Well, whatever your business is, it's no concern of mine. If you follow me I'll show you a room, and you can have it if you like. It'll be a dollar for the day."

"That's fine."

She allowed him to enter, let the storm door slam and led him down a hall.

"I'll need another dollar if you want to take your meals here," she said. "I only have two other boarders now, but I'm cookin' breakfast and supper."

"That sounds fine," he said. "I'll be here for supper, but will probably be gone before breakfast."

Over her shoulder she said, "It'll still be a dollar. If you tell me what time you'll be gettin' up in the mornin' I can have somethin' ready."

Faulkner doubted she'd want to feed him, as by morning everybody in town would probably know what his business had been, but he said, "That's right nice of you, ma'am. I'll be sure to let you know."

She showed him a first-floor room in the back of the house, with a bed, a dresser, an end table and a rocker. Out the back window he could see the land behind the house, flat and empty.

"Will this do, Mr. —"

"Faulkner, ma'am," he said. "Just Faulkner, and yes, this will do fine. Would you like the two dollars now?"

"That would be nice," she said. "I do have to buy some supplies today."

Faulkner took two silver dollars from the pocket of his leather vest and handed them to her.

"Thank you, Mr. Faulkner. I'll leave you to get settled. Supper will be at five — that's about three hours from now."

"Yes, ma'am," he said. "I know what time it is."

"I'm sorry," she said. "I meant no offense."

"None taken. I just didn't want you to think me ignorant."

"I think you're anythin' but ignorant, Mr. Faulkner. I hear the unmistakable sound of an education in you."

"Guilty as charged, ma'am."

"I'll see you at dinner, then."

"Yes, ma'am."

"Oh," she said before leaving, "the hotels in town are not very good, but one of them has a bathhouse. I'd be obliged if you would avail yourself of their services before you get into that bed. I just put clean sheets on it."

"A bath was my very next stop, Mrs. Gentry."

"Well . . . see you at supper, then."

"Yes, ma'am."

CHAPTER 3

Henry Tall Fellow had arranged to meet with Faulkner in Center. It wasn't Faulkner's choice. Their telegrams back and forth had resulted in Faulkner telling him that he had a job in Center. If talking was so urgent that it couldn't wait, then Tall Fellow could meet him there.

Tall Fellow was perfectly aware of what his friend's profession had been for the past twenty-two years. He didn't like to be around Faulkner when his friend was in work mode, but he needed his help badly.

It was past three when the town came into view. Tall Fellow paused before entering town. He'd passed a road sign a mile or so back that had had its population numbers crossed out and changed more than several times. Center did not sound like a town whose fortunes were on the rise, but that didn't matter to Tall Fellow. This was just a stop along the way, a place to meet with

Faulkner and enlist his aid.

Whatever Faulkner had going on in Center, Tall Fellow had no part in it. His plan was to stand aside, let his friend complete his task, and then they'd get out of town and talk.

He gigged his pony into motion and headed for town.

Faulkner came out of the hotel a hell of a lot cleaner than when he'd gone in. He'd slicked back his wet black hair with his hands after a shave and a haircut, and he had turned down an offer of Bay Rum. There was no point in him smelling pretty. He was not a pretty man, and what he had come to town to do was less than pretty.

Faulkner was looking for a man named Robert Cullen. Cullen had killed a woman and her two children down in New Mexico several months earlier. The husband and father, David Victor, had hired Pinkertons to track Cullen down, which they had done. They had tracked him to this little nothing town in Montana. After that, David Victor had needed a man with Faulkner's expertise to finish the job, and he was willing to pay well.

Faulkner's information was that Cullen was holed up in Center — doing what, he didn't know or care. Apparently, Cullen had come upon the Victor ranch and been shown hospitality, which he repaid by raping and murdering the mother, killing the two daughters and then robbing the house. Again, Faulkner did not know or care how Mr. Victor had come up with Cullen's name. He was being paid to do a job, and he was going to do it. Double-checking the facts was not part of it.

There were only two saloons in Center. Cullen had to be at one of them. Faulkner was armed with a complete description of the man, right down to a scar under his left eye. As long as he was still in Center, he would not be hard to find.

Faulkner never spent very much time in a town where he was going to do a job. He did not want people to get used to seeing him, and he certainly did not want anyone to be able to describe him later. Dealing with a livery man or a desk clerk at a hotel — in this case Mrs. Gentry — or a bartender was unavoidable, but beyond that he was able to keep to himself.

Now that he was clean and refreshed and knew he had a place to spend the night, he decided to take one quick look at the town. There was not much going on, and he was able to determine that they had a sheriff,

19

but no deputies. He got most of his information by unobtrusively listening to other people's conversations. In this case there weren't many people available to him, but the people he did encounter were very talkative with each other. For the most part, they talked about getting out of Center and how useless the local lawman was.

It was getting on toward the time of day when the saloons would be busy in most towns. Center was in more trouble than even he had surmised upon riding in. He had not realized that it was virtually a ghost town. He felt bad for Mrs. Gentry and Billy being stuck here. It certainly would not be easy for the woman to sell her house. It was more likely she'd just have to pack up and leave it behind, if she truly wanted to leave.

Faulkner entered one saloon, which boasted four or five customers and a bored-looking bartender. None of the men fit the description of Robert Cullen. He moved on.

The second saloon was grandiosely called the Montana. It was even smaller and less patronized than the first one. About the only thing it had in common with the first was the bored-looking bartender.

There were two customers, one standing at the bar and the other seated. The standing man was portly and definitely not Robert Cullen. The other man sat with his hat on and his head down. Faulkner felt a familiar tickle in his stomach. It was not nerves, because he did not have any. It was that feeling that he'd found what he was looking for.

He looked at the bartender, who had obviously been at his job a long time, because he knew the look. The bartender leaned forward and said something to the standing man, who turned quickly, took one look at Faulkner and then left the saloon.

Faulkner walked to the bar.

"You know that fella?" he asked the bartender.

"I heard some boys call 'im Bob."

"Bob Cullen?"

"I don't know. All I ever heard was Bob."

"You better get out."

"Should I get the sheriff?"

"Just get out."

"Yessir."

"Get me a beer first."

"Yessir."

The bartender drew him a mug of beer, then hurried around the bar and out the batwing doors.

Faulkner picked up the beer and took it with him to the table.

CHAPTER 4

Faulkner sat down at the man's table and set his mug on it. The man looked up and the first thing Faulkner saw was the scar. The second was the haunted look in the man's red-rimmed eyes.

"Bob Cullen?"

Cullen frowned.

"Who're you?"

"That doesn't matter, but my name is Faulkner."

Cullen's eyes widened.

"I know that name."

"Then you know why I'm here."

"I — but you're a — hey, wait. I didn't mean —"

"You should've thought about what you didn't mean before you killed that woman and her daughters down in New Mexico."

"But you — who sent you?"

"The woman's husband," Faulkner said, "the girls' father."

"Look, I didn't mean . . . uh, I mean . . ."

Faulkner sipped his beer and regarded Cullen over its rim.

"Go ahead, tell me what you mean, Bob. I'm listening. We've got a little bit of time."

Bob Cullen sat back in his chair, shoulders slumped, looking defeated. An empty whiskey glass sat in front of him.

"It just got out of hand," he finally said.

"That's it?" Faulkner asked. "That's your defense?"

Cullen shrugged, lifted his arms and let them fall.

"That's all I've got," he said, "except to say that I ain't slept a night since it happened."

"That would be small consolation for the man I work for," Faulkner said. "I can't go back to him and say, 'The man who killed and raped your wife and killed your daughters can't sleep because of it.' That just won't work."

"I know," Cullen said. "I'm ready to go back. I'll give you my gun —"

"No."

"What?" Cullen looked confused.

"I'm not here to take you back, Cullen," Faulkner said. "If you know anything about me you know that's not what I do."

"B-but, I'm givin' up."

23

Faulkner shook his head slowly.

"Sorry." He pushed his chair back. "I'll wait outside."

"B-but —"

"If you go out the back I'll find you."

"There ain't no back way," Cullen said sullenly.

"A window, then," Faulkner said. "Whatever. It's a small town and you'll never make it out."

Cullen's eyes filled with tears, but men had cried in front of Faulkner before, and it didn't work.

"I'll be outside."

"You can't —"

"It's what I do, Bob."

Faulkner turned his back and headed for the door, alert for any movement behind him. It would have been better for both of them if Cullen had tried to shoot him in the back, but he made it to the batwings and then out.

Outside he stepped to the middle of the deserted street, turned and waited. He was prepared to find a lawman waiting for him out there, but that didn't happen. Apparently, the townspeople he'd eavesdropped on were right about the local sheriff.

He watched the batwing doors and just when he thought he might have to go back inside and do it there, Cullen appeared. The man stopped just inside and peered out over the doors. Obviously, he was hoping Faulkner would not be there.

Slowly Cullen opened the doors and stepped out. Faulkner didn't know if Cullen could handle a gun or not, but Faulkner wasn't a bushwhacker, and he wasn't the type to kill an unarmed man. He may have sold his gun for money, but he'd never killed a man who didn't have a fair try at killing him as well.

Cullen stepped outside, let the batwings swing shut behind him.

"Are you really gonna do this?" he asked.

Faulkner didn't answer.

"It's murder, you know."

Silence.

Cullen looked up and down the street, possibly seeking help. There was none.

"Damn you, Faulkner!" he shouted, and went for his gun.

Faulkner was not a fast-draw artist. He'd been outdrawn many times, but he shot straight, unlike other men in the same situation. It took a special talent to be able to draw and fire and hit what you were shooting at. Most men with fast moves had to fire two or three times before they hit their targets. Faulkner was not one of those men.

He always hit what he shot at the first time.

His shot hit Cullen square in the chest. The man had cleared leather, but there was no danger that he might have outdrawn Faulkner. Instead, as he convulsively pulled the trigger, the shot discharged harmlessly into the boardwalk where he stood.

Cullen didn't keel right over. He sort of fell in pieces, folding in on himself, eventually ending up sprawled in the street.

Faulkner holstered his gun, walked to the fallen man, knelt and checked for a pulse. When he was satisfied Cullen was dead, he stood up and looked up and down the street. As far as he could see there had been no witnesses to the event, unless someone was peering out a window. If they were, they weren't coming forward.

Farther down the street he saw a man on a horse riding his way. He could tell from the man's seat who it was, so he stood his ground and waited for Henry Tall Fellow to reach him.

"How do you do that?" Tall Fellow asked, reining in his pony.

"Do what?"

"Your timing," the other man said. Tall Fellow was within a half hour of the time Faulkner had told him to meet him in Center.

"I have my life figured out to the minute."

"Remember me?" Tall Fellow asked. "I've been there when your life was totally out of control."

"Well, that's not the case now."

Tall Fellow looked down at the dead man.

"I take it your business here is done?"

"Oh, yeah."

Henry Tall Fellow stood in his stirrups and looked around. There was still nobody on the street.

"No law?"

"Not much to speak of, apparently," Faulkner said.

"Got a place to stay?"

"Yeah," Faulkner said. "You want a drink first, or a room?"

"Room first."

"Dismount and come with me, then," Faulkner said. "I know a lady and a boy who can use the business."

CHAPTER 5

Mrs. Gentry was very happy to have another boarder. When she walked Tall Fellow to his room Billy accompanied them, but the boy did not get up the courage to speak until they were actually in the room.

"Are you a real Indian?" he asked.

"Billy! Don't be rude," his mother chided.

"No, it's all right," Tall Fellow said. "He's curious. There's no harm in asking." He addressed Billy, who was staring up at him very solemnly. "My father was a Cherokee Indian, but my mother was a white woman."

"Wow! Was she kidnapped by the Indians?"

"No, she wasn't," Tall Fellow said. "My mother was the first woman Indian agent in the West, and that was how she met and fell in love with my father."

"You're really tall. Was your father tall? Was he a chief? Did he take scalps —"

"All right, now that's enough, young

man," Mrs. Gentry said. "You still have plenty of chores to do, and I'm sure Mr. Tall Fellow wants to freshen up and take a bath."

"A bath, ma'am?" Tall Fellow asked.

"Yes," she said, "before you sleep on my nice clean sheets. Mr. Faulkner can show you where."

"Yes, ma'am."

"Supper's in one hour," she said. "If you miss it you'll have to eat in town. I wouldn't wish that on anyone."

"Yes, ma'am."

Faulkner was waiting for Tall Fellow when he came out of the house.

"You didn't tell me I'd have to take a bath to stay at this place," Tall Fellow said accusingly.

"Oh, yeah, I forgot about that," Faulkner said. "She has clean sheets. I'll show you where you can take one."

"Yeah, she told me you would."

"After that we can get a drink."

"She said supper's in an hour and we don't want to miss it," Tall Fellow said. "Apparently it ain't healthy to eat in town."

"I wouldn't think so."

They started walking toward town, having

already put Tall Fellow's pony up at the livery.

"Ain't you worried about having to explain to the law why you killed that fella?"

"I'll deal with that if and when the law even shows up," Faulkner said.

Once again Faulkner waited outside, this time while Tall Fellow took his bath. He refused to allow a barber to cut his long locks, and he also eschewed the use of Bay Rum.

"I almost don't recognize you," Faulkner said when his friend came out.

"Shut up. I need a drink."

"We have time for one, and for a short talk before supper."

They went back to the Montana and saw that the body had been removed from the street out front. When they walked in only the bartender was there, behind the bar.

"You ain't here ta shoot nobody else, are ya?" he asked.

"I've done all the shooting I intend to for one day," Faulkner told him. "My friend and I want a beer."

The bartender eyed Tall Fellow critically. There was still some prejudice against serving Indians in saloons even in 1898, but in the end the bartender couldn't afford to turn away the business. He drew beers and Faulkner and Tall Fellow took them to a table.

"What's so almighty important that you had to meet me here?" Faulkner asked. "You usually stay pretty far away from where I do my business."

Faulkner always found it odd that Tall Fellow disapproved of the way he made his living when their professions were so similar.

"I need your help and I didn't have time to wait," Tall Fellow said.

"Help with what?"

"Does the name Jack Sunday mean anything to you?"

Faulkner sat back in his chair.

"You're going to try for that bounty?"

"It's a lot of money."

"What is it? A thousand?"

"It's gone up," Tall Fellow said. "Twenty-five hundred for him, five hundred for each gang member."

"That is a lot of money," Faulkner said, "but men have tried to bring him in before."

"I know," Tall Fellow said. "Good men. Bryce Benteen, for one."

"He was a good man," Faulkner agreed.

"And Sunday killed him, fair and square, the way I hear it."

"That's how I heard it, too."

31

"If it was only Sunday, or only his men, I'd do it myself," Tall Fellow said, "but the combination is pretty deadly."

"So you want me to help you collect this bounty?"

"For half," Tall Fellow said. "I'll give you half."

"I don't want your money, Henry."

"It ain't even mine until we catch them."

"We'll catch them," Faulkner said.

"Then you'll do it?"

"I'll do it," Faulkner said, "but not for the money. You know that."

"Yes," Tall Fellow said. "I know that."

CHAPTER 6

Supper was a quiet affair. The other two boarders did not seem to like eating with an Indian, but they kept their mouths shut. It may have been the fact that both Faulkner and Tall Fellow wore their guns to the table and were obviously friends.

Mrs. Gentry also did not seem to like the fact that the two men wore their guns, but remained silent about it. Still, the air was filled with tension for everyone but Faulkner and Tall Fellow, who thoroughly enjoyed the meal.

One person was completely oblivious to the tension, and that was Billy Gentry. He chattered on, asking both Faulkner and Tall Fellow questions, and when his mother objected, the two men assured her it was just fine.

"How's the lad going to learn if he doesn't ask questions?" Tall Fellow asked.

Mrs. Gentry was not happy, but she allowed her son to continue to voice his curiosity.

The other two boarders — a drummer and a traveling preacher — finished their meals first and left the table without availing themselves of Mrs. Gentry's dessert.

"That smells like apple pie, ma'am," Faulkner said.

"Would you like a slice?"

"A hunk would be more like it, if that's all right."

"That's fine, Mr. Faulkner. Mr. Tall Fellow?"

"The same for me, ma'am."

"Me, too," Billy said. "I wanna hunk, too."

"And what do you say, young man?"

"Aw, ma," Billy complained. "They didn't say it."

"I know, but I'm not their mother."

Billy looked as if he were going to resist until Faulkner said, "I'm afraid I forgot to say please, Mrs. Gentry."

He kicked Tall Fellow under the table.

"Oh, yeah, me too, ma'am . . . please."

Now all three adults were waiting for Billy to make up his mind.

"Please, Ma, can I have a hunk of pie?"

"Yes," Mrs. Gentry said, "you may all have a hunk of pie. Coffee, too, gents?"

"Yes, ma'am," Faulkner said, then added,

"thank you."

"Yes, thank you," Tall Fellow said.

As she left the room Billy looked at Tall Fellow and asked, "How come you don't talk like an Indian?"

"My mother was a teacher," Tall Fellow said. "She taught me how to speak proper English."

Faulkner knew that Tall Fellow spoke properly until he was angered or provoked, and then his language became a little more like his father's. Although he was half white, it was the Indian part that drove Henry Tall Fellow, along with all its pride and anger.

"Wow," Billy said. "And what did your father teach you?"

"How to be a warrior."

"Wow!" Billy said again. "Can you teach me to be a warrior?"

"Billy!" his mother snapped as she entered carrying a tray.

"Mrs. Gentry, may I answer him?" Tall Fellow asked.

"Well . . ."

"Billy, first of all I won't be around long enough to teach you to be a warrior," Tall Fellow explained, "and second, there's no need for warriors anymore. What you have to do is mind your mama, learn your lessons, and grow up to be a good, hard-

35

working man like your pa. Understand?"

"Yes, sir," Billy said unhappily.

Mrs. Gentry gave Tall Fellow a look that said, "Thank you," as she laid out the pie and coffee, along with a glass of milk for Billy.

But as she turned to go back into the kitchen, she heard Billy say something to Faulkner that really concerned her.

"Mr. Faulkner," he said, "it's all over town how you killed a man today, shot him in the street. Can you teach me to do that?"

CHAPTER 7

Arkansas, 1875

Faulkner knew he needed Henry Tall Fellow, but that didn't mean he had to like the young half-breed.

Basically, he needed him because of his tracking abilities. The Eastern-educated Faulkner had a natural ability with a gun, but he knew nothing about tracking.

"We need some water," Faulkner said.

"I don't," Tall Fellow said.

"When I said we," Faulkner replied, "I meant me and the horses."

Tall Fellow looked up from the hard, dry ground and stared at Faulkner. The two young men had met in St. Joe, Missouri, and discovered they were after the same man, Tom Buckland. Since Buckland was riding with his gang, they had decided to join forces, but they had been rubbing each other the wrong way since the beginning.

"There's a water hole just ahead."

"You know that for a fact?"

"I've been all over Arkansas and the territories, Faulkner," Tall Fellow said. "I know where all the water is."

Tall Fellow went down on one knee, dropping his horse's reins to the ground behind him. Faulkner backed his horse up, so the animal wouldn't cast a shadow where Tall Fellow was examining the ground. He'd only been advised about that once by the half-breed, but he was never a man who had to be told something more than once. It was one of the reasons he'd managed to go through four years of college in two and a half.

"What else do you know?" Faulkner asked.

"I know every inch of this land," Tall Fellow said, "and every town a man like Buckland can get help."

Tall Fellow stood up, walked away from his horse and stared at the ground.

"Do you know enough not to step on a rattler?" Faulkner asked.

"What?"

"Don't move. If you take a step back you'll step on it."

"You better not be kidding, Faulkner."

"It's kind of small," Faulkner said. "I never saw one like that before. It's not even two feet long."

Tall Fellow felt new sweat joining with the perspiration that was already dripping from his chin. It sounded as if Faulkner was describing a pygmy rattler, which, despite their size, were very deadly.

Tall Fellow had to look, and in doing so dragged his heel half an inch — just enough to startle the rattler. It started its death serenade and lifted its head, but before Tall Fellow could do anything, Faulkner drew and fired. The rattler's head flew off, and the body dropped to the ground. The rattle fell silent.

Tall Fellow turned quickly and scanned the ground for any more, then looked up at Faulkner, who was holstering his gun.

"Get in the habit of replacing the spent shells in your gun right away," he said, "before you holster it."

Faulkner stared at Tall Fellow, took his gun back out, ejected the spent shell and replaced it with a live one, then holstered it again. New to the West, he admitted to himself that he could learn a lot from Henry Tall Fellow, but he didn't have to like it.

"You're welcome," he said.

Tall Fellow walked to his horse. The pony was experienced and had not spooked at the sound of the rattler.

As he mounted up Tall Fellow muttered,

"Nice shooting," just loud enough for Faulkner to hear it.

Later that night they camped, built a fire and made some coffee. They were traveling with dried beef jerky and nothing else. Tall Fellow had said they should travel light, and this was one of the first nights since they had left St. Joe a week ago that he was making coffee. Faulkner had almost gotten used to a cold camp.

"Wind's shifted," Tall Fellow explained, "and they're ahead of us. They won't smell the coffee."

"Why didn't we take the snake?" Faulkner said. "I understand you people eat them."

" 'You people'?" Tall Fellow asked.

"I don't mean Indians," Faulkner lied, "I mean Westerners."

"If you're going to stay in the West you're gonna have to stop talking like that."

Faulkner bit off a piece of jerky and said, "You're probably right."

"What's an educated sonofabitch like you doing out here anyway?" Tall Fellow asked. "Weren't you being groomed for banking or politics or something?"

"Both," Faulkner said, impressed that Tall Fellow had been able to guess that.

"What happened?"

"I got disillusioned."

"Why?" Tall Fellow asked.

"They're all thieves," Faulkner said. "I figured if I'm going to deal with crooks I might as well come out here and make a living at it."

"Killing them?" Tall Fellow asked. "That's a living?"

"And what you do is different?"

"I track 'em and take them back for bounty," Tall Fellow said. "That's very different."

"Dead or alive?"

"Usually their choice."

"I don't see that it's so different."

"What do you feel when you kill a man, Faulkner?" Tall Fellow asked. "Or have you even killed one yet?"

Actually, he'd killed four since coming west. The first one was free, but he'd gotten paid for the next three, more each time. It just seemed like an easy way to make a living, and the men he'd killed had deserved it.

"I don't feel anything," he said.

"That's good," Tall Fellow said.

"Why do you say that?"

"If you're gonna kill men for a living," the bounty hunter said, "it's good not to feel anything — otherwise they'd haunt you."

"Haunt me?"

"In your sleep."

"I sleep fine," Faulkner said.

"Again," Tall Fellow said, "good for you."

"Where are we headed tomorrow?" Faulkner asked, changing the subject.

"Rock City is just ahead of us," Tall Fellow said. "I think Buckland is headed there."

"Any law?"

"None," Tall Fellow said. "This territory is covered by federal marshals out of Judge Parker's court in Fort Smith. And he ain't got nearly enough men to cover the area. We'll be on our own — especially if we have to go into the territories. We'll end up facing not only every kind of lowlife outlaw there is, but also some Indians."

"You're an Indian," Faulkner pointed out. "That should help us."

"I'm half white," Tall Fellow said. "That won't be any help at all."

"You haven't got any objection to killing Buckland and his men, have you?" Faulkner asked.

"None," Tall Fellow said. "If that's what it takes. You got any objection to takin' the first watch?"

"None."

Tall Fellow rolled himself in his blanket and turned his back. Moments later he said over his shoulder, "Don't look directly into the fire. It'll destroy your night vision."

Just something else Faulkner would always remember.

CHAPTER 8

When they rode into Rock City, Arkansas, they attracted very little attention, two skinny kids in their early twenties, one a half-breed and the other not much to look at. Faulkner's horse was a nondescript dun; Tall Fellow's horse was a useful mustang that wasn't much to look at.

"This is good," Tall Fellow said to Faulkner. "People aren't really looking at us."

"Jesus," Faulkner said, "people live here?"

The buildings were falling down, many of them had false fronts, and in some places where the buildings had fallen down, tents had been erected in the rubble.

"How long have you been out here, anyway?" Tall Fellow asked, meaning the West.

"More than a year."

Faulkner had killed his first man back east. It was only since he'd come west that he'd killed for money.

"You're gonna see a lot worse than this,"

Tall Fellow said. "You should try living on a reservation."

"That why you talk so well?" Faulkner asked. "You grew up on a reservation?"

"I was educated," Tall Fellow said. "Not college like you, but I had a mother who made sure I was educated."

"A white mother?"

"What of it?"

"Nothing," Faulkner said. "I was just asking."

They reined in their horses in front of the first saloon they came to, the Ruby Palace.

"Not much of a palace," Faulkner said as they dismounted.

"It doesn't have to be," replied Tall Fellow. "We just want a beer and some information."

They tied off their horses and entered the saloon. It was midday and the place was full. No music, a couple of tired-looking girls working the floor, no gaming tables.

"Are they going to answer our questions?" Faulkner asked.

"Why not?" Tall Fellow asked. "We're just a couple of harmless-looking kids."

Back then Tall Fellow was wearing his hair short, a worn hat jammed down on his head. He could pass for white if he had to, and in a saloon he usually had to. It was years later that he started wearing his hair long, with no hat.

They approached the bar and asked for two beers. The bartender eyed Tall Fellow suspiciously, but in the end he served them. It helped that Tall Fellow sounded educated.

"We're lookin' for some boys who rode with Tom Buckland," Tall Fellow said to the bartender.

"You law?"

"We look like law?" Faulkner asked.

"Ya look like a coupla snot-nosed kids gonna get themselves in trouble for askin' after the wrong people."

"That's our business," Tall Fellow said.

"If ya don't mind trouble, ya might try that table in the corner," the bartender said, jerking his chin in that direction. "I think a coupla those boys rode in with Buckland."

"Buckland ain't rode out yet?" Faulkner asked, adopting the bartender's speech pattern.

"He don't check in with me, but last I heard he was still in town."

"Much obliged."

Faulkner and Tall Fellow turned their backs to the bar, leaned on it and scanned the room. There were four men playing poker at the table the bartender had indicated.

"That was pretty good," Tall Fellow said grudgingly.

"Thanks. Sometimes it pays to say 'ain't.' "

"How do you want to play this?"

"I'm looking for Buckland," Faulkner said. "His men are of no interest to me."

"They mean money to me."

"Then you call it."

"We could split up," Tall Fellow said. "You take them, and I'll go look for Buckland."

"Like I said," Faulkner repeated, "these men mean nothing to me. Besides, do we know how many men Buckland has with him?"

"Not exactly," Tall Fellow said, "but certainly more than two."

"So taking these would just alert the others," Faulkner said.

"You make a good point," the half-breed bounty hunter said. "We should find Buckland and take him first."

"I'm going to kill him," Faulkner said. "That's my job."

"By the way," Tall Fellow asked, "who's paying you to kill him?"

"That's my business."

"All right, then." Tall Fellow turned and set down his half-finished beer. "Let's go and find him."

"You're not going to try to stop me from killing him, are you?" Faulkner asked.

"I've seen you shoot the head off a pygmy snake with a split-second draw," Tall Fellow said. "No, I won't try to stop you, but the bounty is mine."

"Agreed," Faulkner said. "I'm getting my pay."

Tall Fellow stared at Faulkner. He almost asked the killer how much he was getting, but decided against it. He didn't want to know if it was more than his bounty.

CHAPTER 9

When they left Center, Montana, Mrs. Gentry was not sorry to see them go. She could have used the money for their rooms had they stayed longer, but she did not like the impression they were making on Billy.

The night before, at the supper table, Faulkner had told Billy, "No, son, I can't teach you to shoot a man down. That you'll have to learn on your own as you get older — if there's even any need for it."

"You don't think there will be?" Billy asked.

"Billy, I think soon there won't be any need for me to carry guns."

The next day, as they rode out, Tall Fellow said, "Last night, what you said about there not being any need for guns?"

"Yeah?"

"You believe that?"

"We're approaching a new century,

49

Henry," Faulkner said. "Yeah, I believe that. Oh, I think there'll be war, and guns to fight the wars with, but the days of a man walking around carrying a gun? Those days will pass."

"And what will that mean to men like us?"

"It'll mean we're old."

Tall Fellow had ascertained that Jack Sunday and his boys were in Colorado.

"You ever hear of Ouray?" he asked. "Red Mountain?"

"Mining towns, weren't they?"

"Once upon a time," Tall Fellow said. "Might still be, for all I know."

"That where they're supposed to be?"

"Supposed to be headed that way. If we don't find them there, we can pick up their trail."

They rode a while in silence and then Tall Fellow asked, "Remember Buckland, Tom Buckland?"

"How could I forget?" Faulkner said. "First time we rode together. I learned a lot from you."

"You know," Tall Fellow said, "you really impressed me the day you shot the head off that pygmy rattler."

"Impressed myself, too," Faulkner said. "I

50

was aiming for the fattest part of that snake."

Tall Fellow looked at Faulkner and said, "I think the head was the fattest part of that snake."

Jack Sunday looked the rancher in the eye when he shot him. He watched the life go out of the man — or maybe that had already happened when he raped the man's wife and his twelve-year-old daughter in front of him. Yeah, maybe the life had already gone out of him.

He turned and looked at his five men.

"Don't just stand there," he said. "Go through the house and take anything of value."

One man was holding the sobbing wife by her arms, pulling them painfully behind her, and another man was holding the strangely quiet daughter around her waist, pulling her body tightly against his. The clothing of both females was in tatters.

"What about these women?" one of the men asked.

"Drop 'em," Sunday said. "We don't kill women."

The two men released the females. The wife crawled to her husband and draped herself over his body, sobbing uncontrol-

51

lably. The daughter simply lay where she fell, unmoving.

"What about us?" asked the man who had been holding the wife. "We get to use the women?"

"No time," Sunday said.

"Can we take 'em with us?"

"What for?" Sunday asked. "There's plenty of whores for you where we're going. Now get goin'," he said. "Search the house, upstairs and down. We got to be on our way."

Another man came in from outside.

"We got the horses, boss."

"The ones I said?"

"Yeah, real good stock."

"Okay, get 'em ready to travel."

Sunday stared down at the crying woman and the catatonic daughter while his men ransacked the house. The daughter might have been worth taking with them, if she were any good anymore, but she seemed to have lost her mind. She was gonna be a pretty one when she got older, prettier even than her ma. But he didn't like that vacant look in her eyes.

Well, whatever happened to her, she'd been broken in.

His men came down with their arms full,

carrying clothes and jewelry. One man had a chair.

"What the hell are we gonna do with that?" Sunday demanded.

"It looks real comfortable."

"You gonna carry that on your horse?"

"Sure, I can ride with it."

"Well, go ahead then, but I'm tellin' you now if it gets in the way it's gonna get left by the side of the road —"

"Okay."

"— along with you!"

CHAPTER 10

Faulkner and Tall Fellow stopped in Denver. Faulkner had not bought a horse in Center. He hadn't wanted to stay in town any longer than he had to.

"This horse is stove in, Mister," Thatcher had told him. "You need a new one."

"I'll pick one up soon," he'd said to the livery man. "Thanks."

"I ain't just tryin' ta make a sale," Thatcher had answered. "I just don't wanna see you get stranded somewhere."

"I'm not riding alone, so that won't happen," Faulkner said, "but thanks." He paid the man more money than he asked for.

As he mounted up to meet Tall Fellow outside the man asked, "Hey, that feller you killed?"

"Yeah?"

"He deserve it?"

"Does it make a difference?"

"It does to me."

Faulkner nodded.

"Oh, yeah, he deserved it."

They stopped in Denver to refresh themselves and to get Faulkner a decent animal. They checked into the Hotel Metropole near the Broadway Theater on 18th Street and Broadway. The desk clerk gave Tall Fellow a look, but apparently had instructions not to turn away any business. Each got his own room.

For the sake of convenience they ate in the hotel restaurant. Luckily, it was one of the best in town. They ordered steaks and caught up on each other's lives since they'd last seen each other over a year earlier.

"You know," Tall Fellow said at one point, "we did this last time."

"Did what?"

"Talked, compared notes, caught up, and you know what?" Tall Fellow asked.

"What?"

"Nothing's changed."

"What did you expect to change, Henry?"

"I don't know, something," Tall Fellow said. "You know how old I am?"

"Forty-five moons?"

"Don't get smart," Tall Fellow said, "but yes, I'm forty-five years old. You know what that makes you?"

"Younger than you."

"Forty-four," Tall Fellow said, "for another few months."

"You remember my birthday?"

"Never mind."

"I don't remember yours."

"It's not important."

"I know. That's why I don't remember it."

"You know, I don't remember you having a sense of humor," Tall Fellow said. "You've always been a dour, dark man — especially in your youth."

"And I don't remember you being so sour on your life," Faulkner said. "Aren't you doing what you want to do?"

Tall Fellow hesitated before answering, played with his food.

"Maybe I'm not anymore . . . maybe. Are you?"

Faulkner shrugged.

"What else should I do?"

"How much longer can you do it?" Tall Fellow asked. "Back in Center you said it yourself. The day of the money gun is coming to an end."

"I didn't say it that way."

"It's what you meant."

"It's still a ways off," Faulkner said.

"Like how far? Six years? The twentieth century isn't going to have room for us, and

56

we'll be fifty then."

"So?"

"Then what?"

"Then nothing."

"What does that mean?"

"It means nothing," Faulkner said again. "We'll be dead, and there'll be nothing."

"So we're gonna be dead in six years?"

"Maybe sooner," Faulkner said. "In fact, I might kill you myself if you keep this up."

"I'm just making conversation."

"Let's change the subject," Faulkner said. "What about dessert?"

Faulkner did not want to think about the future. Lately, he'd been thinking about the past, and that was enough of a waste of time. But at least he knew what had happened in the past. The future was a mystery, and rather than try to guess what was going to happen, he preferred to live it. He knew how old he was; he knew how outdated what he did for a living would probably become. He didn't need to be told those things.

They each had a piece of pie and then Tall Fellow suggested a walk to a saloon.

"Not me," Faulkner said. "I got a nice bed waiting in a real nice hotel room, and I'm going use it. I'll meet you for breakfast in the morning, and then I'll buy a horse and we can be on our way."

"Come on," Tall Fellow said, "one drink. It's early, too early to go to bed. Maybe we'll find some music and girls, or a card game."

"If I go to my room you're still going to go look for those things, aren't you?" Faulkner asked.

"Yes."

Faulkner sighed.

"That means by morning you'll probably be in jail, and by the time I find you and bail you out we'll be behind another day."

"See?" Tall Fellow said. "You have to come with me just to save me from myself."

"Or you could go to your room."

"I'll compromise," Tall Fellow said. "One drink."

"Someplace quiet?" Faulkner asked.

Tall Fellow frowned.

"You don't need a woman tonight, Henry. We have to get going early. Or if you really have to have one, tell the desk clerk. He can probably send one up to your room."

"I like to pick out my own."

"Fine, tell him to send up three and you can pick one."

"Come on," Tall Fellow said, standing up. "A walk to a saloon and a drink."

"No trouble?"

"I promise," Tall Fellow said. He put his hand up and added, "Honest injun."

CHAPTER 11

They walked only two blocks before finding a saloon that Faulkner thought would not offer as many opportunities for trouble as most. There was no music coming from inside, no one staggering around out front, and no loud voices. In addition, all the windows were in one piece.

"I pick this place," he said.

Across the street was a louder, brightly lit, raunchier-looking establishment that Tall Fellow pointed to.

"How about that one?"

"That would be the one if you were actively looking for trouble," Faulkner said. "This is the one for a quiet drink."

Tall Fellow didn't look happy, but didn't balk when Faulkner opened the door, and he followed his friend inside.

The green felt and leather inside still smelled new. Most of the men sitting at tables were wearing suits, and were probably lawyers and bankers. At the bar stood a few common men, wearing normal work clothes that branded them less educated and not as well paid.

Faulkner and Tall Fellow walked to the bar and waved at the bartender.

"What'll ya have, boys?"

"Two beers," Faulkner said before Tall Fellow could order a whiskey. If there was one myth about Indians that Tall Fellow gave credence to, it was that they couldn't hold their firewater.

The bartender came back and set down the two beers.

"You boys are gonna get in trouble for wearin' them guns on the street," he pointed out.

"Is there an ordinance against it?" Faulkner asked.

"Not exactly, but this ain't the Old West anymore, ya know."

"Then I think we'll drink our beer and keep our guns, thanks," Tall Fellow said.

As the bartender went back to the other end of the bar, Tall Fellow shook his head and said, "See? I'll bet they wouldn't bother us about our guns across the street."

"Never mind," Faulkner said. "Drink your beer and let's get back to the hotel."

"This beer tastes like piss."

"When did you turn into such a complainer?"

"It comes with age," Tall Fellow said. "Don't tell me you ain't been complainin' more recently." He took a sip of beer. "You know, things bother me these days that never bothered me before."

"Well, sure," Faulkner said. "You been around as long as we have, something's bound to start bothering you."

Tall Fellow looked around.

"For instance, the way these fellas in their suits are lookin' at us, like we don't belong."

"They're looking at you, Indian," Faulkner said, "and we don't belong."

"Yeah, but they don't know that."

"I shouldn't have even let you sip that beer," Faulkner said. "You're spoiling for a fight. Come on, let's go."

"I ain't finished."

"You're finished." Faulkner took the mug out of his friend's hand. "It tastes like piss anyway. You said so yourself."

"Then let's go across the street and get a good one."

"Back to the hotel," Faulkner said.

He steered Tall Fellow outside and toward the hotel. He wasn't sure what was eating his friend — the way the men in the saloon had looked at him or his advancing age —

but he figured if he could get him back to his room he could avoid trouble — for both of them.

After he deposited Tall Fellow in his room, Faulkner went to his own room. He removed his boots and his gun belt. He checked his poke and saw that he had enough for the hotel and for a horse. There was no need to go to the bank. He had money in several bank accounts, and actually had enough to retire if he wanted to — but retire to what? He could never be a storekeeper or a rancher. Neither was in him.

Tall Fellow had been right about one thing. It was too early to go to sleep. It wasn't even fully dark out yet. He lay down on the bed fully dressed, on his back, intending to close his eyes for a few minutes. Next thing he knew he was being awakened by a persistent knocking at his door, and when he opened his eyes it was pitch black.

He got off the bed and walked to the door and turned up the gas lamp on the wall next to it before opening it. There was a policeman in uniform standing in the hall.

"Can I help you?" Faulkner asked.

"Is your name Faulkner?"

"That's right."

"Do you know a man named Henry Tall Fellow?"

Damn it, Faulkner thought. He knew he should not have left Tall Fellow alone.

"What did he do?" Faulkner asked. "The last I saw of him he was in his room."

"Well, he ain't there no more," the policeman said. He was a broad-shouldered man in his forties, bouncing a nightstick in the palm of his hand while he talked.

"Where is he?"

"Jail," the policeman said. "He says the only person he knows in Denver is you."

"Let me get my hat and my boots and I'll be right with you."

CHAPTER 12

Faulkner didn't like going out without a gun, but he was going to a police station, so strapping one on was not advisable. He had a small gun he used as a hideout, but he left that in the room, as well, just in case they decided to search him.

He accompanied the policeman down to the street where a cab was waiting.

"Nice of you to supply transportation," he said to the uniformed man.

"You're gonna have to pay when we get to the other end."

"Fine."

They both got into the cab, although Faulkner was tempted to tell the policeman to get his own. The man sat across from him, still bouncing the nightstick in his palm. Faulkner assumed he was supposed to be intimidated, but it wasn't happening.

He assumed Tall Fellow must have gone out again after he went back to his own room, and had gotten himself into trouble. Faulkner hoped he hadn't killed anybody.

When the cab stopped, Faulkner paid the driver and followed the policeman up a flight of stone steps into a three-story stone building.

"Wait here," the officer said when they got inside.

Faulkner stood right where he was and watched the policeman walk up to the front desk. He watched as the man spoke with another uniformed officer, this one with sergeant's stripes. The sergeant nodded, then waved at Faulkner to come forward.

"You're Faulkner?" he asked, giving him a hard stare.

"That's right."

"Got any identification?"

"No."

The sergeant stared at him.

"You'll have to take my word for it."

"Your friend got drunk and busted up a saloon," the sergeant said. "Will you stand his bail?"

"Yes."

"What about the damages?"

"They'll get paid." Faulkner would make Tall Fellow pay for it.

"Fine," the sergeant said. "Then I'll take your word that you're who you say you are."

"Believe me, Sergeant," Faulkner said, "nobody would want to claim to be me."

"Bail's a hundred dollars," the sergeant said. "We'll send a bill to your hotel for the damages. You can pay it before you leave town tomorrow."

"Fine."

Faulkner paid the bail and asked for a receipt, just to be difficult. The sergeant handwrote one, then turned to another man and said, "Jensen, go get that Indian."

"Okay, Sarge."

The sergeant looked at Faulkner again.

"You should know better than to let your friend drink," he said. "Indians can't hold their liquor." He accompanied the words with another hard stare.

"He's only half Indian," Faulkner said, "but his white half can't hold it, either."

The sergeant thought that was funny and relaxed a bit. He told the policeman who had fetched Faulkner — and who was still standing by with his nightstick — that he could go.

After that, he gave Faulkner no more hard stares.

When Tall Fellow reached the front desk he saw Faulkner standing there waiting for him. He was still drunk, so his friend seemed to be wavering, but he was there.

"There he is," the sergeant said to Faulkner. "You want him?"

Faulkner eyed his friend critically.

"Do I have a choice?"

CHAPTER 13

Rock City, Arkansas, 1875

"Okay," Henry Tall Fellow said. "Let's leave these two jaspers be for now. Buckland is the big fish we're after."

"Agreed."

"Thanks," Tall Fellow said dryly.

"So should we split up and look for him?"

"You'd like that, wouldn't you?" Tall Fellow asked. "You could find him, take him and claim the bounty."

"I told you," Faulkner said, "I'm not after any bounty. I'm getting paid."

"Yeah, well, money's money."

"Not to me," Faulkner said. "I don't want any bounty money."

Tall Fellow looked at Faulkner, drawing himself up to his full height, from which he looked down on even the six-foot man next to him.

"You'll kill a man for money, but you look

69

down your nose at me for collecting bounties?"

"I'm not looking down my nose at anybody," Faulkner said. "It's just not something I would choose to do."

Tall Fellow waited a few beats, then said, "I can see you and me are just never gonna get on, boy."

"Well, we won't have to after this is done."

Tall Fellow drained his beer mug and slapped the empty down on the bar loud enough to draw attention from the men standing around them.

"Let's take a walk."

The two men at the table who had ridden into town with Tom Buckland were Ralph and Vern. As Faulkner and Tall Fellow left the saloon, the two men playing cards with Ralph and Vern quit and left. It helped that they had lost all of their money.

Ralph and Vern split the winnings between them, even though one of them had won more than the other. That was the nature of their partnership. They shared everything fifty-fifty — which was not the way Tom Buckland operated. That was one of the reasons they were having second thoughts about joining up with him and the others. They had been discussing the subject before the two men had invited them to play poker, and now they took it up again as if they'd never been interrupted.

"And another thing," Vern said. "I don't mind robbin' a bank or two, but I draw the line at killin' for no reason."

"I'm with you there," Ralph agreed.

Vern regarded his partner from beneath the brim of his hat, which he customarily wore at a rakish angle.

"So how do we get away from him now?" he asked. "We've already pulled a few jobs with him. He ain't about to just let us walk away."

"We'll have to bide our time, wait for the right moment," Ralph said.

"It would be helpful if he'd catch a bullet on the next job."

"Yeah," Ralph agreed, "it would be."

They looked at each other, each wondering if the other would actually do it.

Back out on the main street of Rock City, Faulkner and Tall Fellow looked up and down, wondering where to start first. There was plenty of pedestrian traffic as well as a fair number of buggies and buckboards negotiating the street pitted with ruts and holes. Faulkner was starting to realize that Tall Fellow was more comfortable on the trail than he was in town. He'd noticed it when they had met back in St. Joseph, and again here. He didn't like being around a lot of people.

Tall Fellow had been invaluable in tracking Buckland and his gang across Kansas and nearly into Indian Territory. Faulkner thought that perhaps it was his turn to take the lead — if the half-breed bounty hunter was not too proud to follow.

"You got any idea what Tom Buckland looks like?" he asked the bounty hunter.

"Do you?"

"I've got a description."

"I've got a likeness on a poster."

Tall Fellow pulled the poster from his pocket and unfolded it. He handed it to Faulkner, who thought the drawing fit the description he'd been given.

"We should be able to spot him from this," he said, handing it back.

He had the feeling that the reason Tall Fellow didn't split up had nothing to do with the possibility that Faulkner might steal the bounty. He thought it had more to do with Tall Fellow not wanting to walk around town alone.

"Well," Faulkner said, "we might as well get started. How many saloons can there be in town? He's got to be in one of them. Failing that, we can check hotels."

"And whorehouses," Tall Fellow said. "My information is that he definitely likes whorehouses."

"Okay," Faulkner said, "maybe whorehouses before hotels."

"So," Tall Fellow said, "do you really think we should split up?"

"No," Faulkner said. "We might run into him while he's with other members of his gang. It's probably safer if we stay together."

If the suggestion relieved Tall Fellow, he didn't allow it to show. They started walking. Rock City was not a large town, and it wouldn't take long to walk from one end to the other.

"How much do you know about Buckland?" Faulkner asked.

"I know he rode with Bill Doolin's Wild Bunch for a while," Tall Fellow said. "Lately he's gone out on his own, put his own gang together, and started hitting banks. And I know he's either very brave or very stupid."

"How so?"

"Look where he's holed up," Tall Fellow said. "We ain't so far from Fort Smith, where Judge Parker sits on the bench. Buckland's thumbing his nose at him."

"Then Judge Parker will be real happy when you bring him in."

Tall Fellow didn't comment.

Faulkner knew that Buckland and his gang were hitting banks. He was being paid by a bank president to track and kill Buckland. The one bank teller Buckland had killed while robbing the bank had been the man's wife.

"What about the Wild Bunch?" Faulkner asked.

"What about them?"

"Ever tracked any of them?"

"I leave Bill Doolin and his men to Marshal Bill Tilghman," Tall Fellow said. "Those fellas have a history I don't want to get involved in."

"Have you met Tilghman?"

"No," Tall Fellow said, "and I don't know that I want to. I don't think he likes bounty hunters very much." After a moment Tall Fellow added, "And he probably likes hired guns even less."

"Thanks for the warning."

They made a circuit of the town, stopping in three saloons. The decided it wasn't very smart to come out and ask bartenders if they had seen Buckland or any of his gang. Word might reach the outlaw before they did.

They did, however, ask one bartender the

location of the whorehouses in town.

"You young fellas lookin' ta get yer ashes hauled, huh?" the man asked.

"Something like that," Faulkner said.

The man gave them two locations, and advised them on which whore to ask for at each.

"Guess you must go pretty often," Faulkner said.

"You kiddin'?" the man asked. "It's the only place I can get away from my wife."

They found Buckland at the second whorehouse. When they got in and talked with the madam, they pretended to be his men.

"We need to find our boss," Tall Fellow said. "Is he here?"

"He's been here for days," she said with distaste, "and he's tearin' through my girls. Two of them can't work for a week, and one of them left me. Can you get him out of here?"

Suddenly she seemed to realize she was talking to two of his men. Her hand went to her mouth and she said, "I'm sorry, I didn't mean —"

"Relax," Faulkner said. "We're not really his men."

She dropped her hand and looked at them with interest.

"Are you here to take him away?"

"Yes," Tall Fellow said.

"Not exactly," Faulkner said.

Tall Fellow looked at the woman and said, "I'm here to take him in; he is here to kill him."

"I don't care which one you do," she said, "as long as you get him out of here."

"What room is he in?" Tall Fellow asked.

"One," she said. "Top of the stairs."

"Any of his men up there?" Faulkner asked.

"No, just him and one of my girls, Elena. You'll try not to shoot her, won't you?"

"We'll do our best," Faulkner said.

"I mean," the woman said, "if you have to shoot her to get him I guess you could, but —"

"We won't shoot her," Tall Fellow assured her.

"Anyone else up there?" Faulkner asked.

"There are two more rooms in use," she said. "The other girls are in the parlor."

"Keep them there," Faulkner said. "And you stay there with them."

She went into the parlor and they could hear her telling the other girls that two men had come to take away Buckland. The girls cheered, but she shushed them.

"How do you want to do this?" Faulkner asked.

"Well," Tall Fellow said, "I want to take him, but you want to kill him. I guess you should go in first. If he kills you, then I'll take him."

Faulkner didn't know if Tall Fellow thought he was being funny, but to him it sounded like a good plan.

"Okay then," he said, drawing his gun. "Let's do it."

CHAPTER 14

1898

Faulkner tossed more bacon into the frying pan, then poured two more cups of coffee and reached across the fire to hand one to Tall Fellow.

They had left Denver early that morning, Tall Fellow in an evil mood because he was hungover and sore. Hungover because he had sneaked out after Faulkner left him in his room and gone to that other saloon. Once there he had ordered a bottle of whiskey and commenced drinking it. Three quarters of the way through, he had gotten into a fight with three locals who didn't like having an Indian in their place. By the time the police came, Tall Fellow had the three men out cold on the floor and had thrown a chair through the mirror behind the bar. The police had waded in with their nightsticks . . . which was the reason he was sore.

He didn't talk during their ride, and

Faulkner did not try to get him to talk. Something was bothering his friend, and he was going to leave it to Tall Fellow to tell it when he was ready.

"Thanks," the bounty hunter said, accepting the coffee. He sipped it and said, "I'm sorry."

"For what?"

"I cost you money," he said. "I'll pay you back for the bail and the damages."

"Yeah, you will," Faulkner said. "As soon as we can get you to a bank."

"Don't worry," Tall Fellow said. "You'll get it."

"I'm not worried."

When the bacon was ready Faulkner doled it out and handed Tall Fellow a plate and a fork.

"Don't you want to know what happened?" the half-breed asked.

"I know what happened," Faulkner said. "The police told me what happened."

"Don't you want to know why?"

"That's up to you."

"So you're not going to ask?"

"You want me to ask?"

"No."

"Then I'm not," Faulkner said. "You'll tell me . . . if and when you're ready to."

They ate in silence, and then Tall Fellow

said, "You've always been a good friend, Faulkner."

"Yeah, well . . . so have you, Indian."

They finished eating and had some more coffee. Then they rolled themselves up in their bedrolls.

"Maybe tomorrow," Tall Fellow said.

"What?"

"Maybe tomorrow I'll tell you."

"Go to sleep, Indian."

Jack Sunday reined in his horse, but signaled to the rest of his men to keep going. He turned and watched the straggler. His name was Jerry Hobbs and he was struggling with that damned chair he'd taken from the ranch house.

When he reached Sunday he also reined in.

"Drop it," Sunday said.

"What?"

"Drop the damned chair."

"Aw, Jack —"

"Drop it or I'll drop you," Sunday said. "Your choice. You're slowin' us down."

Hobbs looked at the chair, which he was having trouble balancing. It was upholstered with green and gold threads and he really liked it, but realistically speaking, when was he ever going to get a chance to sit in it?

And he sure didn't want to die over it.

He dropped it.

"Now catch up to everyone else, Hobbs."

"Right, boss."

Sunday looked down at the chair, lying on its side in the dirt. It reminded him of the ranch and what had gone on there. He allowed himself a moment to smile, then rode on to catch up with the others.

"What makes you think we're even on their trail?" Faulkner asked.

"I have a friend says he saw Jack Sunday in Denver," Tall Fellow said. "And that he and his men were going to head south."

"South? Southeast? Southwest?"

"South," Tall Fellow said. "He's going to look for a place to hole up until the heat's off. Probably a small town. Maybe an old mining town."

"Sounds like a lot of guesswork to me."

"A lot of my work is guesswork, Faulkner. Don't worry. We'll come across something that tells us we're on the right track."

"Like what?"

"Knowing the reputation of Sunday and his gang," Tall Fellow said, "probably something like that."

He pointed into the distance, where black smoke curled up into the air.

"That's a wood fire," Faulkner said.

"And a big one."

"A house?"

Tall Fellow nodded.

"A house, a barn." He looked at his friend. "Maybe even a whole ranch."

They headed that way to take a look.

CHAPTER 15

When Faulkner and Tall Fellow reached the fire they saw that they had been right. It was an entire ranch that was burning — house, barn, bunkhouse, corral. Men from a nearby town and some neighboring ranches were battling the inferno, but to no avail.

"Should we help them?" Tall Fellow asked.

"It's a lost cause, Indian," Faulkner said. "Let's find out if anyone knows how it happened."

They dismounted, walked over to where a potbellied man with a badge was standing. He was too old and fat to fight the fire, but that didn't keep him from barking orders.

"Looks like a lost cause," Tall Fellow commented.

The lawman looked at him, then at Faulkner, but didn't say anything.

"Anybody know how it started?" Faulkner asked.

"Not by accident, that's for sure," the lawman said. "We pulled Hank Foley and his family out. He'd been shot; his wife and daughter had been raped and killed."

"Daughter?" Faulkner asked.

"Twelve," the sheriff said. "It looks like her parents had been killed, but they left her alive. That didn't stop them from settin' the place on fire, though. The girl wouldn't leave her folks."

"Was she injured?"

"She was . . . slow," the lawman said. "Not right in the head, and bein' raped didn't help. No, she wasn't so injured she couldn't have got out." He looked at the two of them. "She just stayed with her folks and the smoke killed her even before the fire could get to her."

"Jesus," Faulkner said.

"What about the bunkhouse?" Tall Fellow asked.

"Empty. This family had fallen on hard times. They didn't have much, but that didn't keep them from being robbed and killed."

Tall Fellow was examining the ground. Even accounting for the men fighting the fire, he could see that there had been a gang there.

"Anybody see the gang that did it?"

The sheriff looked at Tall Fellow again.

"Folks over at the Emery place saw a bunch of riders go by. If they didn't have a bunch of hands over there with guns, they might've been the ones who got hit. So instead, they kept going until they got here. They also stole some stock out of the corral."

He paused to shout some more orders, but the men were starting to back off now. He turned and looked at Tall Fellow.

"Who you trackin', bounty hunter?"

"Jack Sunday and his gang," Tall Fellow said, not wondering how the lawman knew what he did for a living. "This looks and sounds like their work, right down to the stolen stock."

"Well then, you must be on the right track."

"I guess so."

Now the sheriff looked at Faulkner.

"You a bounty hunter, too?"

"No."

"Well, you ain't law."

"No."

"Then that'd make you a money gun."

Faulkner shrugged.

This time the lawman turned and faced them. His eyes were streaming. Could've been from the smoke, Faulkner thought. Or maybe not.

"Normally, I don't hold with bounty hunters or hired guns," he said, "but I'm tellin' you boys I wish you luck. Track them sonsofbitches and kill them all."

"You formin' a posse?" Tall Fellow asked.

"Yeah. I'm from over in Forsythe, a little ways from here. I ain't gonna get much more than some ranchers and merchants."

"If we stop to join you we'll fall behind," Tall Fellow said.

"I know that," the lawman said. "Just go, track 'em to hell if you have to — and Money Gun?"

"Yeah?"

"Put one in Jack Sunday's head for me, and for this family."

CHAPTER 16

While the other men vainly fought the fire, trying to save whatever they could, Tall Fellow walked the grounds, examining the dirt for tracks. It was hard, because the gang had not only ridden their own horses, but had stolen stock as well. Tall Fellow had to try to separate the gang horses from the tracks the firefighters' horses made.

"How we doing?" Faulkner asked, coming up alongside him.

"I think I got them isolated," Tall Fellow said. "See there? The stock they stole are not shod. They're gonna leave an easy trail to follow."

"Good," Faulkner said, "let's follow it."

Tall Fellow looked over at the sheriff and the firefighters. The fire was going out, more by itself than from anything the men had done. The wood was beginning to smolder.

"Shouldn't have done that to the little girl," he said.

"Hey, Indian," Faulkner said. "Wasn't it you who taught me that you and I can't afford personal feelings in our business?"

"Yeah, but . . . a little girl, and she wasn't even right in the head." He looked at Faulkner. "That wasn't right, Faulkner. Did she even know what was happening to her?"

Faulkner slapped his friend on the back and said, "Track 'em, and we'll ask them."

They mounted up, took a last look at the tableau they were leaving behind, then rode off.

As they left the ranch behind, the tracks became easier for Tall Fellow to see. He seemed to find particular characteristics for one of the shod horses and one of the unshod horses. Faulkner could tell the tracks of a horse with shoes from the ones without, but anything more individual than that escaped him. He remembered how impressed he'd been by Tall Fellow's skills the first time they'd met — not that he would have admitted it back then. They had both been much too full of themselves to admit anything like that — even though Tall Fellow did admit later that he was impressed with Faulkner's ability with a gun. Later in their friendship Tall Fellow said if they could have combined their talents, they would have been the perfect bounty hunter. Faulkner never really appreciated the observation.

"How far ahead?" Faulkner asked.

"Judging from the tracks and the fire, a day," Tall Fellow said. "Those boys were fighting that fire for a while, and it burned hot. They were too late to do any good when they got there."

"How'd they know about the little girl, then?"

Tall Fellow shrugged.

"Maybe the father lived long enough to drag her to safety. Or the mother. Who knows?"

Faulkner looked at the sky.

"Might as well camp here," he said. "You can't track them in the dark."

Tall Fellow looked up.

"I could with a better moon."

"The horses need rest, anyway," Faulkner said. "I'll build the fire." He handed Tall Fellow the reins of his horse. They may not have ridden together for a while, but they fell into their familiar roles. Faulkner made camp; Tall Fellow cared for the horses.

They sat around the fire, drank coffee and ate dried beef jerky. Some things never changed, Faulkner thought. Whenever they were tracking someone they traveled light, coffee and jerky really being the only necessities. With beef jerky they were able to make cold camps when they needed to.

"I'm gettin' old," Tall Fellow said.

"We're all getting old, Indian."

Apparently, his friend was ready to talk about what was bothering him. Faulkner allowed him to get to it in his own time.

"You know, there was a time I could have tracked these jaspers in the dark," Tall Fellow said. "But those times are past."

Faulkner didn't comment. There was something else coming.

"You remember the first time we rode together?" Tall Fellow asked.

"Tom Buckland."

"Yeah, Tom Buckland."

More silence.

"You remember the way you shot the head off that pygmy rattler?" Tall Fellow asked.

"Scared the shit out of you."

"That was some shot," the half-breed said. "Man, you could've shot the eye out of that snake, and I could see sign for miles."

"I remember." Faulkner thought he could still shoot the eye out of a rattler, but he kept quiet. This wasn't about him.

"I can't see so good anymore."

"What?"

Tall Fellow waved his hand in front of his face.

"My eyes. Not so good anymore."

"What are you saying?"

"I went to a doctor," Tall Fellow said. "Supposed to be pretty good one, too."

"And?"

"And . . . he says within five years I'll be totally blind."

"Well, crap," Faulkner said.

"Yeah," Tall Fellow said, "that was pretty much my reaction, too."

CHAPTER 17

Rock City, Arkansas, 1875

Faulkner went up the stairs first, followed by Tall Fellow. Upstairs they could hear voices — a man yelling, a woman crying out in either pain or pleasure. When they reached the top they could tell that the voices were not coming from the room Tom Buckland was in.

They stepped to the door, taking up position on either side. Before they could move, a man came out of the room across from them, hitching up his pants and carrying his gun belt. He stopped short when he saw the two men standing there holding guns.

"What the hell?" he shouted, and inexplicably went for his gun.

"Damn it!" Faulkner felt he had no choice. The man was grabbing for his gun with bad intentions. Faulkner shot him dead center, driving him back into the room. At the same time, Tall Fellow kicked open the door of room one and ducked inside.

Faulkner followed him in, but all they saw was a skinny, naked girl on a bed.

"He went out the window," she yelled, pointing.

Neither man was distracted by her tiny breasts and bony hips, and they both rushed to the window.

"I'll go," Tall Fellow said.

"I'll take the front."

The second-floor window led to a low roof above an alley. Faulkner sprinted down the stairs, hoping he'd catch Buckland coming out of the alley.

Nobody got between Faulkner and the front door until he came charging out and ran into two middle-aged women carrying packages. He tried to avoid them, but while he did manage to miss running into then, he scattered their packages all over the street.

"That horrible, horrible place!" one of them shouted.

When Faulkner reached the alley it was empty.

"Tall Fellow!" he shouted.

Holding his gun ready, he entered the mouth of the alley, eyes and ears ready. There were a lot of possibilities. Buckland could have been hiding somewhere in the alley — there were doorways, crates and barrels — or he could have beaten Faulkner to the mouth of the alley. Maybe he didn't even come down the alley. Tall Fellow could have been chasing Buckland behind the buildings. Faulkner quickened his pace, ready for Buckland to jump out at him. It didn't happen. He reached the back of the alley and was now underneath the window.

The skinny whore leaned out the window. Faulkner suddenly noticed how pale her skin was, and how dark brown her nipples appeared. She was not an attractive girl.

"They went that way," she said, pointing.

Sure enough, Tall Fellow was chasing the outlaw behind the buildings.

"Where does that lead?" Faulkner asked.

"If you keep on goin' you'll get to the livery stable."

He waved with his left hand and began to run with his gun still held in his right. Tall Fellow would be in trouble if Buckland managed to get to some of his men.

Ralph and Vern left the saloon and started walking toward their hotel. They were across the street from the whorehouse when a man came bursting out, knocking packages from the hands of two women.

"Ain't that where Buckland is?" Ralph asked.

"That is where Buckland has been since we got here," Vern said.

"Wonder what's goin' on?" Ralph asked.

The man looked around, then turned and went into the alley next to the building.

"He's chasing somebody," Ralph said.

"Maybe he's going to solve our problem for us," Vern said.

"Where are the others?"

"I don't know," Vern said.

"Well . . . what do we do?" Ralph asked.

"As far as I'm concerned," Vern said, "we can just wait."

Faulkner kept running, alert for the sound of shots he hoped he wouldn't hear. He wanted to catch up to Tall Fellow before any shooting started. He probably should have gone out the window right after the bounty hunter.

This was one of the reasons he had chosen a profession where he would be able to work alone. He always thought having a partner would be more trouble than it was worth. Here was a perfect example. Without Tall Fellow he would have been the one going out the window, and he'd be in pursuit of Tom Buckland.

Where was that goddamned Indian, anyhow?

CHAPTER 18

1898

When they woke the next morning, they had coffee in silence. Faulkner stole glances at his friend, as if now that he knew, maybe his eyes would look different, but they didn't.

"What about a second opinion?" Faulkner asked.

"Had one," Tall Fellow said. "Went to San Francisco to see a specialist. He confirmed what the other sawbones said. No hope. In five years my eyesight will be totally gone."

They fell silent again, until Tall Fellow said, "You know what good a blind tracker is?"

Faulkner shrugged. He knew that if he ever went blind he'd put his gun to his head and pull the trigger. Tall Fellow, being the same type of man he was, would probably do the same.

"I'll get the horses."

Faulkner kicked the fire to death, then stowed the coffeepot in his saddlebags. When Tall Fellow came over with the horses, they each saddled their own and mounted up.

"Looks like they're headed for the mountains," Tall Fellow said. "Might be wanting to hole up in a mining town like Red Mountain or Ouray."

"Well, you're on their trail," Faulkner said. "They're not going to get away."

"No," Tall Fellow said, "they're not."

"What is this place?" Hobbs asked.

"It's called Ouray," Sunday said. "The mines here are playin' out some, but the town's hangin' on. It's a good place to stop over."

Ouray had never experienced a fire like the ones that had wiped out many other mining towns. This was the 1900s and there were families living there, unconvinced that the mines would play out completely. The railroad had almost come in once or twice, and there was still some hope that would happen, as well.

"There law here?" Hobbs asked.

"Far as I know," Sunday said. "We're here to lie low, though. Pass the word that any man starts trouble, I'll kill 'im. I want a good night's sleep and we all get out of here in the mornin', nice and peaceful."

"Gotcha, boss."

"That means you, too, Hobbs. Understand?"

"I said I gotcha, boss," Hobbs said, looking hurt.

"Just wanted to make sure."

They rode into town without the horses they had stolen. They were able to sell those along the way and make a pretty penny for them. Sunday figured he could keep his boys in check until morning. He'd let them loose on the next likely ranch they came to. He wanted to keep Ouray as a place he could go when he just needed to eat, drink and sleep. No trouble.

There had to be one place like that for a man like Jack Sunday to go, didn't there?

"How far is hooray?" Faulkner asked.

"It's Ouray," Tall Fellow said. He pronounced it "yer-ray."

"Well, how far?"

"We could make it there tonight, if we have some luck."

At that moment luck did strike them, but it was bad. Faulkner's horse suddenly took a bad step and almost went down.

"Whoa!" Faulkner said, dropping to the

ground immediately. He lifted the horse's front right leg, then dropped it. "This stupid sonofabitch stepped on something."

He was pissed not because he had become attached to the horse, but because he had just paid good money for the animal in Denver.

"What was that you said about luck?" he asked, looking up at Tall Fellow.

"There are some ranches up ahead," Tall Fellow said. "We might be able to pick up a mount there."

"I hate having to pay for another damn horse," Faulkner said.

Tall Fellow dismounted and took a look at the horse's hoof.

"It's bad, but not permanent," he said, dropping the hoof to the ground. It never got there. The animal kept it lifted. "I'll bet you could trade it and just throw in a little cash."

"I suppose so."

"Come on," Tall Fellow said. "We'll walk him so we don't do any more damage."

"So much for getting to hooray tonight," Faulkner said.

"Ouray," Tall Fellow corrected. "It's yer-ray."

"Yeah, yeah . . ."

■ ■ ■ ■

"There," Tall Fellow said an hour later. "A ranch, and a fairly good-sized one."

"It's not on fire," Faulkner said. "That's encouraging."

"Maybe they bypassed it because they'd already burned one down and killed the family that lived there. Maybe Jack Sunday just likes to do one of those a day."

"Might play havoc with a man's digestion, huh?"

"Not a man like Sunday."

"You talk like you know him."

"I just know the name," Tall Fellow said, "but I know him better now that I heard what he did to that little girl."

They started down the hill toward the ranch.

CHAPTER 19

As the men approached the ranch house they could see that the corral was full of horses. This was good news for Faulkner — as long as the owner was willing to part with one.

Their approach was noticed by several men who were milling about the house and barn. None of them were armed. As they reached the house one man broke away from the others and approached them. Faulkner noticed two or three men moving toward what appeared to be a bunkhouse, and figured they wanted to be close to their guns, just in case. One man stepped into the barn and came out holding a rifle. Faulkner didn't feel threatened, though. He was sure it was just a precaution on their part.

"Afternoon," the man said. "Help ya?"

"I hope so," Faulkner said. "My horse went lame. I was hoping I could buy one from you — maybe trade."

"Well, we got plenty of horses," the man said. "What's wrong with yours?"

"Looks like a stone bruise," Tall Fellow said.

The man nodded.

"My name's Christian," he said, with no indication of whether it was first or last. "I'm foreman here."

"You got the authority to sell?" Faulkner asked.

"I do," Christian said. "I'll have my man look at your horse while you look over our stock and pick out one you like. Then we can talk price."

Christian waved and another man came over.

"Unsaddle this man's horse and check the animal out. He may be using it to trade as partial payment for a new mount."

"Okay, Chris."

The other man led the horse toward the barn.

"Let's go over to the corral."

The three of them walked over, Tall Fellow still leading his own horse. When they reached the corral, he tied the horse's reins to it.

"Good-looking stock," Faulkner said.

"We pride ourselves on raising good

horses," Christian said.

"Mind if I go in?"

"Go ahead, pick yerself out a good one."

"Henry?" Faulkner was always careful not to call Tall Fellow by his Indian name in front of others.

The two men opened the corral gate, entered and closed it behind them. They walked among the horses.

"See," Tall Fellow said right away, "this is what I'll miss when I'm totally blind."

"What's that?"

Tall Fellow pointed to the ground. All Faulkner saw was a jumble of tracks, hoofprint atop hoofprint.

"I don't see it."

Tall Fellow stooped and pointed.

"There."

Now Faulkner saw it.

"Is that the track we've been following?"

"One of them," Tall Fellow said. "These fellas bought the horse from Jack Sunday."

"What do we do now?" Faulkner said.

"There's no brand on the horses," Tall Fellow said. "Probably because the guy had no ranch hands. Maybe he was going to hire some and brand the stock, but it wasn't done."

"So we can't prove these are stolen horses."

"No."

"Well," Faulkner said, "I need a horse, and you need to catch up to Jack Sunday. Let's just buy a horse and keep moving."

"I wonder if these men — this man, Christian — knew they were stolen? Or is he just trying to impress his boss with a corral full of horses when he gets back?"

"Doesn't matter to us, Indian," Faulkner said. "Once we catch Sunday we can send a telegram, if you want, tell that sheriff where he can find these horses. Let him determine if they're stolen, and then take legal action."

Tall Fellow thought a moment, then said, "Why not? We've already lost enough time."

"Then help me pick out a horse and let's get back on the trail."

They did not choose one of the best horses in the corral because Faulkner did not want to pay top dollar.

"You always scrimp on your horses," Tall Fellow complained. "That's why you go through so many."

"I just need four legs and a back to sit on," Faulkner said. "Hey, maybe if we tell them we know they're stolen we can buy even cheaper."

"Never mind," Tall Fellow said. "We're not taking the best, but let's not take the worst."

They decided on a six-year-old mare who looked like she'd have a good wind.

They pointed out the horse to Christian, who nodded.

"Not bad," he said. "Not one of the best, but not bad. Eddie tells me your horse is pretty sound except for the stone bruise. I think we can come to a fair price."

They talked a while and Faulkner paid what Tall Fellow would later say was not a fair price.

"It was worth it to me not to have to dicker," Faulkner would say. "I hate dickering."

"You would've made a horrible horse trader."

"Thank God."

"I'll need my bridle," Faulkner told Christian, who sent a man to the stable to fetch it. He slipped the bridle over the mare's head and led her from the corral. Eddie took her to the barn to saddle her while Faulkner and Christian closed the deal.

"You fellas got time for a drink?"

"We've got to get on our way," Faulkner said.

"Who you trackin'?"

Faulkner and Tall Fellow exchanged a look. "Who says we're tracking anybody?'

"You just got the look."

Faulkner glanced around. The men who had gone to the bunkhouse had strapped on guns. Several other men had retrieved their rifles. He had the feeling if Christian thought they'd figured out that the horses were stolen, they would be in trouble.

"We just have to keep moving," Faulkner said.

He knew the remark gave the impression that they were being tracked, not doing the tracking, but that seemed best at the moment. He got a look of approval from Tall Fellow that only he was able to read.

Eddie brought the horse back out, saddled and ready to travel. He handed the reins to Faulkner.

"There ya go," he said.

Faulkner wanted to check his saddlebags, but decided not to do it in front of them. Besides, there wasn't much of value in them to be stolen — an extra shirt, a backup gun, a coffeepot. If they wanted any of those things, they were welcome to them.

They both mounted up and started their ride out, turning to exchange a wave with Christian.

"A lot of guns for a ranch," Tall Fellow said.

"An odd ranch," Faulkner said. "They buy

stolen horses and claim to have raised them."

"I wonder if there even is an owner," Tall Fellow said. "That Christian shows a little more authority than a foreman should."

"Even more reason to have a lawman come back and check this place out," Faulkner said. "Maybe from the next town?"

"Don't know how much law there is between here and Ouray," Tall Fellow said. "But we can send a telegram. Maybe a federal marshal."

"Let's move a little faster before they change their minds," Faulkner suggested, and they both gigged their horses into a canter, then a trot, and then a full run.

CHAPTER 20

The extra stop to buy a horse kept them from reaching the town of Ouray that day. They actually camped at the base of the San Juan Mountains, with intentions of continuing in the morning.

Once they started up the mountain, it would be difficult to find tracks on the hard ground. They had to hope that Sunday and his gang had, indeed, continued on to Ouray and not taken a detour somewhere along the way.

Faulkner would have bet a lot that his friend could track a mouse through a snowstorm. But with his announcement about his eyes, they would probably have to depend a little more on luck than they usually did.

"We better stand watch in case they decide to double back this way," Tall Fellow said.

"You figure they're expecting a posse?" Faulkner asked.

"I'm hoping they're going over this mountain to avoid one," the half-breed said. "A posse of an overweight sheriff and a bunch of store clerks is not going to track a gang over a mountain."

Faulkner poured a cup of coffee for Tall Fellow and handed it to him, then one for himself.

"That was good," Tall Fellow said.

"What?"

"You didn't mention my eyes."

"It's not for me to mention," Faulkner said. "They worked pretty good in that corral back there."

"Yeah, some days they work just fine. Other days . . . and at night . . . I never know what it's going to be like."

"I can stand the first watch," Faulkner said.

"That might be best," Tall Fellow said. "It will be darkest then. You will see better than me."

In Ouray Jack Sunday met in a saloon with Hobbs and a few of the other men. Of the twelve men who rode with him, four were present. These were his core four, as the others came and went — sometimes killed in action, other times killed by him in a fit of rage.

"I've decided where we are goin' from here," he said to the men.

"Where's that, Jack?" Eddie Hall asked.

"Gunman's Crossing."

They all exchanged a glance.

"Have any of you been there?"

The men shook his head.

"Have you been there, Jack?" Hobbs asked.

"No," Sunday said, "but I'm lookin' forward to it. If it's everything we hear it is, it'll be a place for us to rest for a bit."

"I thought that's why we were here," Hobbs said.

"Here?" Sunday asked. "There's one damn saloon here, and no whorehouse. And not a decent restaurant. No, Gunman's Crossing is where we'll be able to get back —"

He stopped short.

"Get back what, Jack?" Hobbs asked.

"That's all," Jack Sunday said. "We'll be leavin' at first light. Tell the other men."

The four exchanged glances once again.

"Get out!" Sunday shouted.

Other patrons looked over as the four men stood and left Sunday to sit alone.

Jack Sunday needed to get back the fire he usually felt in his belly, the edge he usually lived on. Gunman's Crossing — a

111

notorious, legendary home for outlaws. But part of the story of Gunman's Crossing was that anyone wishing to stay there had to pay for the right.

Sunday was going to have to come up with a pretty good score between Ouray and Gunman's Crossing in order to raise the money. One last score before taking a restful leave from the robbing and stealing and killing that defined Jack Sunday's life.

CHAPTER 21

In the morning Henry Tall Fellow woke Faulkner and handed him a cup of coffee.

"No more after this," he said. "The fire is already out."

"Just as well. We should get going."

Faulkner rolled out of his bedroll and got to his feet.

"Can I ask you something?" Tall Fellow asked.

"Sure."

"How are you are hired?" Tall Fellow asked.

"What do you mean?"

"How do people know what you do?" Tall Fellow asked. "How do they know where to find you?"

"Word of mouth," Faulkner said.

"So whoever it is hired you to kill Jack Sunday just tracked you down, person by person, until he found you?"

"Exactly."

"It sounds . . . painstaking."

"If someone wants to hire my services bad enough," Faulkner said, "they find me."

They saddled their horses, climbed aboard and headed up the mountain.

The San Juan Mountains were beautiful, but the same could not be said for Ouray. Mining towns did not aspire to beauty, but to functionality. In its time Ouray had functioned just fine. Someday they might see prosperity again. At the moment the town was hanging on, trying not to go the way of most mining towns. That was because, for the most part, it was not inhabited by the transients who were attracted to most mining towns — the gamblers, the merchants, the thieves, pimps and whores — who knew in their hearts that their stay was temporary, until the next big strike was hit.

Ouray was inhabited by miners, merchants and their families, whose intent was to stay and to grow with the town.

However, when Faulkner and Tall Fellow rode in, all they saw was a mining town on the verge of death. Later, in their absence, it would rise again as new minerals were discovered in the mines. For now, the rutted, muddy streets were empty, and the smell of panic and despair hung in the air.

They rode up to the saloon, dismounted and tied their horses to a rickety post.

"Gone," Tall Fellow said.

"The town?" Faulkner asked, thinking his friend was advancing an opinion.

"Sunday and his men," Tall Fellow said. "They wouldn't stay here more than a day. There's nothing here for them."

"Well," Faulkner said, "if they were here, this is the place to find it out. Why would they come here and not go to the saloon?"

"Agreed."

They approached the ramshackle building that housed the saloon and entered. Inside it was empty due to the early hour. What miners were left were hard at work. A bored-looking bartender stood up straight as they entered, maybe just in anticipation of having something to do.

"Help you gents?"

"Two beers and some information," Faulkner said.

"I got both for ya," the barman said. He drew the two beers and laid them on the scarred, pitted bar in front of them. "There's your beer. What's this information you need?"

"We're tracking about ten or twelve men led by an outlaw named Jack Sunday," Tall Fellow said.

"Well, let's see . . ."

"This is a yes or no question, my friend," Tall Fellow said, cutting him off. "Were they here or weren't they?"

"There was a bunch of fellers in here yesterday, and I do believe I heard one of them be called Jack. So I guess the answer's . . . yes."

"And where are they now?"

"That I don't know," the bartender said. "They left town this mornin'." He shrugged. "Could be anywhere by now."

Faulkner sipped the beer, then turned his head and spit it out onto the floor.

"I think I know why they left."

"Yeah, I know. Ain't very good. Yer better off with whiskey."

Faulkner did not want Tall Fellow to get started drinking whiskey, so he said, "No, that's okay. We have to be on our way."

"You gonna follow them fellers?"

"We are," Faulkner said.

"Bounty hunter?"

Tall Fellow asked, "Why?"

"Well, seems to me a bounty hunter might be willing to pay for a little . . . information?"

"What kind of information?" Tall Fellow asked.

The bartender hesitated.

Tall Fellow took a dollar out of his pocket and placed it on the bar.

"That's all?"

"Until I hear the information," Tall Fellow said, "I won't know what it's worth, will I?"

The man picked up the dollar and put it in his own pocket.

"Them fellers had a conversation last night about where they was goin' from here. That worth more?"

Tall Fellow put another dollar on the bar. The bartender picked it up and put it in the same pocket as the other one.

"They mentioned Gunman's Crossing."

Faulkner and Tall Fellow exchanged a look.

"But there ain't such a place for real, is there?" the bartender asked.

Tall Fellow put five one-dollar pieces on the bar and he and Faulkner walked out.

"What do you think?" Tall Fellow asked when they reached the horses.

"Why not?" Faulkner asked. "It's as good a place as any for them to go to lie low for a while."

"Yeah, but we don't want Jack Sunday lying low," Tall Fellow said. "I want him in a cell, and you want him dead."

"I guess that means we're going to Gunman's Crossing."

"You ever been there before?"

"No," Faulkner said. "You?"

"No. You believe there actually is a place called Gunman's Crossing?" the bounty hunter asked.

"If there is," Faulkner said, "a man would have to be crazy to go there."

"And two men would have to be even crazier to follow ten or twelve there," Tall Fellow added.

"You got any idea where it is?" Faulkner asked.

"I got an idea."

"Can we take a shortcut, maybe get there ahead of them?"

"From here?" Tall Fellow shook his head. "We're just gonna have to take their trail from here. No way we can get ahead of them."

"We're gonna be braced as soon as we ride in," Faulkner said. "We're going to need a story."

Tall Fellow mounted up and said, "We got time to come up with one, don't we?"

CHAPTER 22

1875

Faulkner ran virtually the length of Rock City before he reached the livery stable. When he got there it was quiet, no movement at all. He crept closer, gun ready, wondering what trouble that Indian had gotten himself into.

He had two ways to go, the front or back of the stable. He could see people walking by out front, so he turned and walked toward the back. Behind the building he found a horse trough, a corral, and an unconscious Henry Tall Fellow.

He rushed to the bounty hunter's side, still alert for a trap. With his gun in his right hand, he reached out with his left to find a pulse while continuing to look around. Nobody jumped out at him or took a shot, and at that point the half-breed groaned.

"Hey, Tall Fellow?" Faulkner said, shaking the man. "What happened?"

Tall Fellow rolled onto his side and squinted up at Faulkner.

"I don't know. Everything just went dark."

"You hurt?"

"I don't know."

"Sit up." Faulkner reached out his left hand to help Tall Fellow into a seated position. "Check out your parts."

Tall Fellow wriggled his arms and legs, found them sound and working.

"I don't seem to be wounded, but I have a helluva headache." He felt the back of his head. "Ow."

"Bump?"

"Not yet. Kinda pulpy."

"Yeah, you'll get a bump. Can you get up?"

"Yeah."

Again, Faulkner gave him his left hand, this time pulling him to his feet. Tall Fellow started looking around.

"Try the trough," Faulkner said.

"Huh?"

Faulkner pointed.

Tall Fellow searched the ground a little longer, then walked to the trough and plunged his hand in. Moments later he came out with his gun.

"How'd you know?" he asked Faulkner.

"It's what I would have done."

"And would you also have let me live?"

"No," Faulkner said. "If it was me I would have killed you while you were lying on the ground."

"I guess I'm lucky it wasn't you."

"You'll have to clean and dry that gun," Faulkner said. "My bet is Buckland is gathering up his men."

"I guess the element of surprise is gone," Tall Fellow said.

Faulkner, finally satisfied that nobody was going to start shooting at them, holstered his weapon.

"We better get back to our hotel," he said. "We're going to need more guns."

"Let's do this quick," Tall Fellow said. "They may come after us, or they may leave town. We better be ready for both."

They headed for their hotel.

When Ralph and Vern saw Tom Buckland they both cursed softly.

"Where you runnin' to, Tom?" Ralph asked.

"Coupla bounty hunters just tried for me at the whorehouse," Buckland said. "We're gonna need the rest of the boys to take care of them."

"You sure they were bounty hunters?" Vern asked.

"Bounty hunters, lawmen, it don't make no difference," Buckland said. "We gotta get rid of them."

"Why don't we leave town?" Ralph asked.

"Because I ain't ready ta leave town," Buckland said. "I cold-cocked one of 'em but he ain't gonna stay out forever."

"Why didn't you kill 'im?" Ralph asked.

"Because his partner was on my tail," Buckland said. "Where are the rest of the boys?"

"One of the saloons, I guess," Vern said.

"Well, you two split up and find 'em," Buckland said.

"Where are you gonna be?" Vern asked.

"I'm gettin' my rifle," Buckland said. "Get the rest of the boys and meet me in front of the rooming house."

"Okay," Ralph said, exchanging a look and a nod with Vern.

"Okay," Vern said.

When they got back to their hotel, Faulkner went to his room for his rifle, then came back down the hall to Tall Fellow's room.

"Dry that gun out?" he asked.

"Later," Tall Fellow said, holding up another handgun. "I've got an extra one." He holstered it and grabbed his rifle. "Let's find those sonsofbitches."

As Faulkner and Tall Fellow came down

the stairs, two armed men walked through the front door into the lobby. They immediately covered them with their rifles.

"Hold up," Vern said, putting his hands in the air. "We're just here to warn you."

"About what?" Tall Fellow asked.

"Buckland and about six of his men will be at a rooming house at the north end of town," Ralph said.

Both Faulkner and Tall Fellow recognized these two from the saloon. The bartender had pointed them out as two of Buckland's men.

"And why aren't you two going to be there with them?" Faulkner asked.

"We don't want to be part of any killing," Ralph said.

"You're two of Buckland's men, aren't you?" Tall Fellow asked.

"We want out," Vern said.

"That's right," Ralph said.

"We ought to take you in right now," Tall Fellow said.

"You can do that," Ralph said, "but you'll probably miss the others."

"And Buckland's the one you really want," Vern said. "There's more money on his head than the rest of us combined."

"You're better off lettin' us go and goin' after them," Vern said.

Tall Fellow looked at Faulkner, who said, "I'm after Buckland, remember? You can take these guys to the jail and turn them over to the sheriff. Collect your reward."

"While you go and face Buckland and the rest?" Tall Fellow asked. "Get yourself killed? How could I live with myself if that happened?"

Faulkner looked at Ralph and Vern.

"I guess you boys lucked out," he said. "Get out of town and don't let us see you again — ever."

"Don't worry," Vern said. "You won't."

"We're goin' straight," Ralph said. "There's too much killin' involved in stealin'."

CHAPTER 23

1898

"We fell farther behind than we thought," Tall Fellow said, studying the ground.

Faulkner looked down from his horse. He never bothered to dismount for two reasons. One, he never saw what Tall Fellow saw, and two, he didn't want his friend to think he didn't trust his eyes.

"How'd we do that?"

"We didn't," Tall Fellow said, climbing back into the saddle. "I may have misread the sign."

"The bartender in Ouray only put us a few hours behind."

"Well," Tall Fellow said, "somehow it's gotten stretched to about half a day."

"Still not bad," Faulkner said. "If we start pushing we can catch up."

"That's part of the problem," the bounty hunter said. "It looks like they're pushing."

"In a hurry to get to Gunman's Crossing."

"I was hoping we might have a chance to catch them before they got there."

"We'll just have to go back to the original plan," Faulkner said. "Track them there and take them there."

Tall Fellow sat still in his saddle.

"What is it?" Faulkner asked.

"Doesn't it occur to you that I might get you killed?" his friend asked.

"That's occurred to me quite a bit over the years," Faulkner said.

"But I mean now . . . especially now."

"Sure, it occurred to me," Faulkner said, "but you asked me for my help. What was I supposed to do?"

"But I wasn't fair to you, Faulkner," Tall Fellow said. "I didn't tell you everything. I didn't tell you about my eyes."

"Well, now I know," Faulkner said, "and the longer we sit here talking, the farther behind we're getting."

"I just wanted to tell you, if you want to pull out now, there's no hard feelings."

"I'm not pulling out."

"I just wanted to give you the chance."

"Well, you did," Faulkner said. "Thanks."

"You're welcome."

Faulkner pointed ahead of them and said,

"Gunman's Crossing."

"Yep," Tall Fellow said. "Gunman's Crossing."

Late in the day they came to a town called Milner. It was a fair-sized town, visible from miles away, and as they got closer they decided they'd stop there for the night.

"Might as well," Faulkner said. "It's here, so is dusk, and we could use some coffee."

Tall Fellow didn't argue.

But as they entered Milner something felt wrong. People on the streets pointed at them and got off the streets. They didn't walk, they ran. And there was something in the air, something tangible, real, not a feeling.

"Burning," Faulkner said.

"Yeah, something was definitely burning around here," Tall Fellow agreed.

And then they saw it. The other buildings were all intact, some older than others, some very recently erected. Milner seemed to be a town on the rise — only it didn't have a bank anymore, because somebody had not only burned it down, they'd obviously blown it up.

"Oh, hell," Faulkner said as a group of men wearing badges and carrying rifles appeared ahead of them.

CHAPTER 24

"They look mad," Tall Fellow said.

"If we go for our guns there's going to be a bloodbath," Faulkner said.

"So what do we do? Turn and run?"

"Then they'd start shooting for sure," Faulkner sad. "We're going to have to talk to them."

"Okay," the bounty hunter said, "but about what? What are they mad at us for?"

"We're about to find out."

Faulkner and Tall Fellow stood their ground and waited as the group approached. They became aware of people behind curtains and windows, staring out, watching. And the street had cleared. There was only the two of them, plus the eight or ten lawmen approaching.

As the group came closer Faulkner spotted one man in the front and decided to key in on him. He looked the most comfortable wearing the tin star.

Remembering Tall Fellow's eyes he said, "Thick-set fella in the front, looks like the sheriff."

"I got him," Tall Fellow said. "The rest look like a posse, not used to wearing the star."

"I think Sunday and his gang hit the bank," Faulkner said, "and these boys want to take it out on us."

"That ain't fair," Tall Fellow said.

"Let's see if we can convince *them* of that."

Sheriff Evan Tucker eyed the two strangers like they were his salvation — and maybe they were. The town fathers were up in arms. They wanted his badge and his head — not necessarily in that order — because of the gang who had robbed the bank, taking every cent in the vault while blowing up the building, killing two people in the process.

All he had to do was convince everyone that these two strangers were part of the gang. If he could at least put two of the gang in jail — or in the ground — it might save his job. All he had to do was convince these part-time deputies — who had all been deputized after the fact — to go along with him.

Holding his shotgun tightly in his hands,

Tucker stopped his makeshift posse in front of the two men and glared up at them. He didn't know who they really were, but it didn't matter. As far as he was concerned, they were part of the gang. If he could convince himself, he could convince anyone.

"You boys got a lot of nerve comin' back here!" the sheriff said to Faulkner and Tall Fellow.

"We don't know what you're talking about, Sheriff," Faulkner said. "We just got to town."

"A little too late to split the booty with your partners, eh?" the man said.

"Booty?" Tall Fellow asked. "What booty?"

"Look at 'em," the sheriff said. "Actin' like they're all innocent."

"Uh, Sheriff," one man said. "Maybe they are innocent."

"What are ya talkin' about, Lew?" the sheriff said. "Don't you think it's a coincidence that two strangers ride into town right after a bunch of 'em rob the bank? These fellas obviously got here too late to help their buddies."

"Uh, yeah," the man called Lew said, "and that would make 'em innocent, Sheriff."

"It don't make 'em innocent," the sheriff argued. "It makes 'em part of the gang that

130

got here too late to help their buddies —
but they know where they are!"

A few of the other deputies liked that logic
and started nodding in agreement.

"Sheriff, if we were part of a gang who
just robbed your bank, and we were too late
to be in on it, wouldn't we be pretty stupid
to ride into town? Especially since we can
see the bank's been hit."

"Then that's what you are," the lawman
said. "Stupid."

Faulkner looked at Lew, pointed to him.

"You sound like a smart man, Mister," he
said. "You don't believe that, do you?"

"It don't matter what he believes," the
sheriff said. "He's a goddamn storekeeper.
I'm the law around here."

"Sheriff," Tall Fellow said, "you've got to
be a pretty piss-poor lawman if all you can
do after your bank is robbed is accuse two
innocent men. Why didn't you stop them
when they were robbing it?"

"That's what a lot of folks are wondering," Lew said.

"And if they're gone, and you've got this
posse, why aren't you on their trail?" Faulkner tossed in.

"We were headin' out when you rode in,"
the sheriff said. "Now that we got you, you
can tell us where they're headed."

131

"We've got no idea, Sheriff," Faulkner said, "because we're not part of the gang. As a matter of fact, if it was who we think it was, we've been trailing them for some time."

"Who do you think it was?" Lew asked.

"The Jack Sunday gang," Tall Fellow said.

"You fellas ain't lawmen," the sheriff said.

"No, we ain't," Tall Fellow said.

"Bounty hunters?" Lew asked.

"I said you were a smart man," Faulkner said. "That's it exactly."

"Sheriff," Lew said, "at least these two fellas are tellin' who robbed the bank."

"Course they are, damn it!" the sheriff snapped. "Because they were supposed to be in on it."

"Nobody believes that, Sheriff," Tall Fellow said.

"You're just trying to save face at our expense," Faulkner said, "and we ain't about to let you do that."

"Whataya gonna do about it?" the lawman asked. "Yer outgunned, Mister."

"By you and a bunch of storekeepers?" Faulkner asked. "I don't think so, Sheriff."

"These men are duly appointed deputies."

Faulkner ignored the sheriff and addressed the other men.

"How many of you boys want to die

because your sheriff is trying to save face? And his job?"

The men muttered among themselves, exchanging glances.

"Mister," Lew said, "maybe if you told us your names it'd help."

"I'm nobody," Tall Fellow replied, "but maybe you heard of my partner, here. . . . His name's Faulkner."

Faulkner didn't know if any of the deputies recognized his name, but he could see by the look on the sheriff's face that he did.

"Wait a minute," one of the men said. He was standing at the back of the group of deputies, and pushed his way to the front. "I know who this fella is. He ain't no bounty hunter. He's a money gun."

"You're right," Lew said. "I know that name, too, and he ain't never been a bank robber that I know of."

"So what?" the sheriff said. "He's a hired killer. That makes him better than the bank robbers? I say we take him, anyway."

"You've got no wanted posters on me, Sheriff," Faulkner said. "I don't want to go up against the law, but I'm not about to let you take me down for something I didn't do."

"Me, neither."

"You a money gun too, Mister?" Lew asked.

"He is a bounty hunter," Faulkner said. "His name's Henry Tall Fellow, and he brings most of his bounties in dead."

"And you're after the bounty on Jack Sunday's head?" Lew asked.

"That's right."

"Seems to me we'll be doing your lawman's job for him," Faulkner said. "Killing Jack Sunday and his boys, and bringing back your money."

"That sounds good to me, boys," Lew said. "I don't aim to go against these fellas with a gun."

"You're yella, Lew," the sheriff said.

"And where were you when your town's bank was being robbed, Sheriff?" Tall Fellow asked. "Under your desk?"

The harsh words pushed the sheriff into action. He started to bring the shotgun around, but he found himself staring down the barrel of Faulkner's gun. The sheriff had left Faulkner no choice but to draw, despite the fact that the movement might have also pushed some of the other men into action — but it didn't. They were all stunned by the speed with which Faulkner had produced his gun.

"He coulda killed you, Sheriff," Lew said.

"He coulda killed you easy."

"I told you I didn't want to go against you, Sheriff, but you're not leaving me much choice," Faulkner said. "It's your play."

CHAPTER 25

Faulkner knew he was facing a man with a badge, but he wasn't willing to be pushed. All he and Tall Fellow had done was ride into town, and this clown with a tin star on his chest was trying to save his job by blaming them for the bank robbery. He could count the times he'd drawn on a lawman on one hand, and he had only killed one over the years — a bad one. This one wasn't bad, really, just desperate and stupid. But Faulkner was ready to not only draw on this one, but to kill him if he had to.

It was the man's own choice.

Henry Tall Fellow had never killed a lawman, but he was ready to back his friend's play. He didn't care if only the sheriff drew, or if all nine of the men in front of them drew (he had counted). He had been angry ever since the day his eyes had been diagnosed. So far all he'd done about it was get drunk and start fights, like in Denver. Maybe today was the day he took out his anger on someone and killed him.

This idiot with a badge was asking for it.

Sheriff Evan Tucker knew he'd bitten off more than he could chew. How was he supposed to know that one of the strangers riding into town was a famous gunman and killer, accompanied by a bounty hunter? He stared up at the two men on horseback and knew that even if he got lucky and killed one of them, the other one would kill him. He had no doubt that they would target him before anyone else in the group. It was what he would do, kill the leader first.

And there was no guarantee that any of the other men with him would even make a move.

Jesus Christ, he thought, it's just a fucking job!

"So go ahead, Sheriff," Faulkner said. "Make a decision."

Both Faulkner and Tall Fellow thought that the lawman could probably use a way out, but neither one was in the mood to give it to him. The moron had put his foot in his mouth; let him swallow it or spit it out.

"Well," Sheriff Evan Tucker said, "maybe

I made a mistake."

"Maybe you did," Faulkner said.

"Put your guns up, boys," the lawman said. "These men ain't part of the gang."

Faulkner and Tall Fellow saw all of the men roll their eyes. They had never raised their guns.

"Sheriff," Lew said, "if these two men are trackin' the Sunday gang I don't think you need any of us anymore."

"Maybe you're right, Lew."

"You should probably just ride along with them."

The sheriff turned and looked at Lew as if he were crazy.

"That's okay, Sheriff," Tall Fellow said. "We usually work better with just the two of us."

"You men go on back to your businesses," Sheriff Tucker said. "Drop your badges off at my office later."

He didn't have to tell them twice. Three of the men took their badges off right away and handed them to him.

"Sorry about this," Lew said to Faulkner and Tall Fellow as the other men drifted away. He stepped closer and said, "My name's Lew Hilton. I'm a member of the town council."

"When did the Sunday gang hit?" Faulkner asked.

"Late yesterday," Lew said. "The first we knew of what was happening was when the bank blew up."

"How many killed?" Tall Fellow asked.

"Two," Lew said. "A teller and a woman who was making a deposit."

"How many were there?" Faulkner asked.

Lew looked at Sheriff Tucker.

"Ten, twelve," the lawman said.

"You get a shot off?" Tall Fellow asked, already knowing the answer.

"Uh, no," the sheriff said. "I was, uh, in my office . . . workin'."

Asleep was more like it, Faulkner thought.

"You boys want to come over to the saloon I'll stand you to a drink," Lew Hilton said. "Make up for the . . . mistake."

"We don't have time," Tall Fellow said. "We've been tracking these boys for a long time now."

"Where you figure they're headed?" Lew asked.

Faulkner knew that Tall Fellow — who was, after all, after the bounty — would never answer a question like that.

"Don't know," he said.

"We're tracking them," Tall Fellow said.

"Well," Lew said, "you need any supplies before you leave?"

"Some," Faulkner said.

"Come on over to the general store and I'll get you a good price on what you need."

"That going to be okay with the owner?" Faulkner asked.

"No problem," Lew Hilton said. "That's me."

CHAPTER 26

Lew Hilton not only gave them supplies at a cheap price but poured them each a shot of whiskey to cut the dust. They declined a second drink and packed the supplies they'd purchased into their saddlebags. They would have liked to stop for a hot meal, but that would only put them farther behind Sunday and his gang. They were acting on the assumption that the bartender in Ouray had heard right and the outlaws were on their way to Gunman's Crossing, but there was always the chance that they weren't. There was always the chance they might catch up to them in the open somewhere.

Saddlebags filled with bullets, coffee, bacon, beans and celebratory cigars that the man had thrown in free — "To light up when the job is done" — they mounted up in front of the general store. Hilton and the sheriff watched them from the boardwalk in front of the store. Then, suddenly, a group of men closed in on them from all sides. These were men with guns, no badges, and bad intentions.

"What's going on?" Sheriff Tucker demanded.

Faulkner and Tall Fellow might have been able to gig their horses and ride through the group, but not without shots being fired. They exchanged a glance that said, "We thought we were done with this," and waited.

"We heard you caught two of the gang that robbed the bank," one man called out.

"That was a mistake," Lew Hilton shouted back, doing the sheriff's job. "These men are not part of the gang. They're trackin' the gang."

"They said that?" a second man called.

"And you believed 'em?" a third added

"Yes," Hilton said, "the sheriff and I believe them."

"So you're just gonna let 'em ride out, Sheriff?" someone shouted.

"That's right," the sheriff said. "When they catch up to the gang they'll recover whatever money they can and bring it back here."

Faulkner, getting tired of being accused, wasn't so sure he would do that. Once they caught up to the gang, who was to say where recovered money came from?

"I think we ought ta keep 'em here and question 'em some more," someone said.

"Nice friendly little town you got here, Mr. Hilton," Faulkner said.

Hilton moved closer to Faulkner.

"They're good people," he replied. "They're just scared and upset. Many of them lost their life's savings in the robbery."

"All the more reason they should let us go and get it back," Tall Fellow said.

"You have to get these people to move, Mr. Hilton," Faulkner said. "We don't want to have to shoot our way out of this town."

"Just let me talk to them," Hilton said, stepping away to address what was becoming a mob. If any more men joined in, there would be far too many for Faulkner and Tall Fellow to successfully shoot their way out.

"People, people," Hilton shouted, raising his hands. "Nothing will be accomplished by detaining these two men except to let the gang get farther away."

"That's what you say!" somebody said.

"The sheriff and I have determined that these two men are who they say they are."

"The sheriff's an idiot!"

"And you're no lawman!"

Different voices were joining in now.

"I say we go ahead and lynch 'em!"

Suddenly it got quiet, as if the statement had shocked everyone into silence.

Faulkner drew his rifle from its scabbard and Tall Fellow followed.

"We're not about to sit here and let anyone hang us for something we had no part of," Faulkner called out. "You men outnumber us, but how many of you have ever killed a man?"

There was no answer.

"And how many of you are willing to die so the others can hang us?" Tall Fellow asked.

Again, there was no answer.

Tall Fellow levered a round into the chamber of his rifle, and this time it was Faulkner who followed.

"Make a move," Tall Fellow said, "or make a path."

There was plenty of tension in the air as each member of the mob examined his own conscience, and courage, and stupidity. One by one they began to move aside, until suddenly there was a path.

"Good thinking," Faulkner said. "Tall Fellow, you go ahead. I'll bring up the rear."

Tall Fellow started down the path and Faulkner followed, but turned in his saddle so he could keep a watch on the crowd in

case somebody got brave.
   Nobody did.

CHAPTER 27

"What the hell is wrong with people?" Henry Tall Fellow asked.

They were camped, hours later, with a pan of beans on the fire, cups of coffee in their hands.

"They're either stupid or scared," Faulkner said, calmly.

"I think we just ran into a town full of people who are both."

Tall Fellow shook his head and sipped his coffee.

"You know," he said, "two other men would've just started shooting and taught them a lesson."

"You're probably right."

"In fact," the bounty hunter went on, "there was a time we would've taught them a lesson."

"The townspeople don't make me as mad as the sheriff," Faulkner said. "How does someone who is that much of a moron wind up wearing a badge?"

"Probably because nobody else wanted it."

"That's a job I'd never want," Faulkner said. "I don't know of a more thankless job than town sheriff or marshal. You see those folks who were backing him? None of them ever would've lifted a gun against us."

"Yeah, but that mob later. Somebody there would've started shooting if you hadn't talked them out of it. You're good with words, Faulkner."

The beans were ready and Faulkner dished them out, handing a plate to Tall Fellow.

"But you know," Tall Fellow continued with a mouthful, "I really wanted to shoot somebody today."

"I know."

"You knew?" Tall Fellow asked. "How?"

"I can feel it in you, Henry," Faulkner said. He rarely — if ever — called his friend by his first name. "You're angry, and unless you get it under control, somebody's going to pay for it."

Tall Fellow chewed, washed his food down with coffee, then held the cup out to Faulkner.

"I've got a right to be angry," he said, as Faulkner handed the cup back.

"I know you do," the money gun said.

After a moment Tall Fellow added, "But I guess somebody else shouldn't have to pay for it."

Another moment of silence went by and then Faulkner asked, "Yeah, but who should?"

CHAPTER 28

1875

Ralph and Vern had delivered Tom Buckland's message to his men before they went to the hotel to find Faulkner and Henry Tall Fellow. Everything was set for them all to shoot it out with each other while Ralph and Vern left town.

Naturally, they hoped that the two bounty hunters would come out on top, but even if Buckland survived, they would be long gone. And they were going to find themselves a small town that nobody had ever heard of, where he'd never find them.

Faulkner and Tall Fellow knew that Ralph and Vern had to have their own reasons for warning them, but they didn't care. Faulkner's job was to kill Buckland, and the bounty on these two men — if there was one — was of little interest to Tall Fellow.

They were both interested in Buckland

first, and anyone else second.

Buckland waited in front of the rooming house for his men to arrive, which they did, mostly two at a time. Before long he was standing there with seven men. The only two missing were Ralph and Vern.

"What happened to them?" one of the other men asked.

"It don't really matter," Buckland said. "They were never really part of the gang anyway, were they?"

"They never did join in on any of the fun," another man said — and by fun he meant raping and killing.

"So what's goin' on?" a third man asked.

"Bounty hunter," Buckland said. "Almost caught me with my pants down at the whorehouse."

"We lightin' out?"

"No, we ain't lightin' out," Buckland said. "You better all check yer guns and make sure they're workin'. We're gonna kill us some bounty hunters."

"Anybody we know?" a man asked.

"No," Buckland said. "From what I saw, it's a coupla kids tryin' to make a name for themselves."

"Too bad," one of the gang said. "I'd like to kill me a famous bounty hunter."

"Well," Buckland said, "we'll kill us these two, and then find you a famous one to kill. How's that?"

The other man grinned, showing tobacco-stained teeth, and said, "I like the sound of that!"

As inexperienced as they were — relatively speaking — the thing Faulkner and Tall Fellow had in their favor at that time was their youth. As impetuous as it made them, it also made them fearless.

However, that didn't mean they were going to go rushing in without having a look first.

"How many?" Faulkner asked.

"I count nine."

"That's what I get. Spot Buckland?"

"On the porch," Tall Fellow said. "He has the demeanor I've seen on the old chiefs."

"You're comparing Tom Buckland to a chief?"

"No," Tall Fellow said, "obviously not. I just meant the way the others are staying together it's obvious he's in charge."

"Oh . . . I can see that."

"Also," Tall Fellow said, "I've seen him once before."

"Fine," Faulkner said. "How do you want to do this?"

"If we go walking in there they'll just start shooting."

"How about the local law?"

"We might lose them."

The were standing alongside a building, their backs to the wall. Faulkner peered around the corner.

"No horses," he said. "It doesn't look like they're going anywhere." He turned back and looked at Tall Fellow. "I think they're waiting for us."

"No," Tall Fellow said. "They don't know we know where they are."

"Unless those other two sent us into a trap?"

Tall Fellow thought a moment, then said, "No, I believed them. They wanted to get away from Buckland. They're hoping they can get away while we are all shooting at each other."

"Okay, that makes sense to me. You got any suggestions?"

"I've got one."

"And?"

"We let them come find us."

CHAPTER 29

1898

Jack Sunday and his gang rode into Gunman's Crossing as if they were entering a church.

"There ain't no law here at all?" Hobbs asked.

"None," Sunday said. "The only law here is what you're wearin' on your hip."

They kept riding until they reached a livery stable.

"I didn't see no bank," a man named Harry Wells observed.

"Why would there be a bank here?" Sunday asked. "Somebody would just rob it."

Hobbs laughed and added, "Every damn day!"

They all laughed then, until Sunday shut them up.

"This is like any other town, minus the bank and a lawman wearin' a star," he told them, "but I'll kill the first man I hear talkin' about what we do, understand? We took a nice chunk of money out of that last bank. Anybody in this town hears about it, they'll try to take it away from us."

"But . . . we're all the same here, ain't we?" Hobbs asked.

"If by that you mean we're all thieves and killers," Sunday said, "the answer is yes — and remember that. Any man here would just as soon kill ya as look at ya."

"What about us?" a Mexican named Soul asked. Sunday found the man's name ironic, because he doubted that Soul had one.

"Whataya mean?" Sunday asked.

"Can we kill anyone, *jefe*?"

"You can kill or rape anybody you want," Sunday said. "Just don't expect me to back you up. You can back each other up, but every man here is responsible for his own life. You wanna back each other up, that's fine. Just don't come runnin' to me to pull your bacon out of the fire if you fuck up."

"What if one or more of us wants to leave?" Danny Barker asked.

Barker was the only college-educated member of the gang. He had come west after school, looking for adventure, and Sunday found him to have less conscience than any man he'd ever met. At twenty-three he had a lot of killing ahead of him. It was too bad he'd come along this late in the century, though. Sunday wished he'd had Barker around ten or twenty years ago.

"Any man wants to leave can go ahead and do it," Sunday said.

"With our share?"

"No," Sunday said. "We divvy up after we leave here together. If you leave, you leave with what you have in your pocket."

"That ain't fair," Hobbs said.

Sunday stared at him.

"You wanna take that up with me now, Hobbs?"

Hobbs hesitated, looked around to see if he had any supporters, then said, "No."

"Anybody else?" Sunday asked, just to make sure.

The men all looked at each other, then said, "No," or shook their heads.

"Good. Let's get our horses taken care of. Then it's up to all of you to find your own rooms. You wanna do that in a hotel, a boarding house, a saloon or a whorehouse, I don't care."

"If we're all on our own," Barker asked, "how will we know when you're ready to leave?"

"Don't worry," Sunday said. "I'll let you know when it's time to leave."

CHAPTER 30

Tall Fellow became morose nearly every night when they camped. He was okay during the day, unless he got very quiet. That was when Faulkner knew he was starting to stew, so he'd start up a conversation to try to distract his friend from his thoughts.

Sometimes, though, like this afternoon, Tall Fellow felt the need to talk, and Faulkner obliged him.

"You know, they say Hickok's eyes were failing him when he was killed," the bounty hunter said.

"I heard that," Faulkner said. "I never did hear that it had anything to do with him getting killed, though."

"No," Tall Fellow said, "but what do you think his life would've been like if he hadn't been killed that day in Deadwood? He was a scout, a gunman, a gambler . . . what good would he have been at any of that without his eyes?"

"I guess he would've gotten himself killed sooner or later, then."

Tall Fellow paused for a while, then said, "Reckon that's what I'll do, then. Keep tracking and hunting until I get myself killed."

Faulkner took a moment to think before answering, "I guess that's what I would do, too, Indian."

"There is no sense in going out the way Doc Holliday did," Tall Fellow said. "Flat on his back in bed in a nursing home."

Faulkner shuddered at the thought of dying that way.

"What about —" he started to ask, then thought better of it.

"What about what?" Tall Fellow asked. "Go ahead, Faulkner. You're the only friend I've got. If you can't say it, nobody can."

"I was just going to ask, what about eyeglasses?"

"I talked to a doctor about that," Tall Fellow replied. "He said it might help for a while, but my eyes will continue to get worse and I'd have to keep changing the glasses."

Once again Faulkner considered the prospect of losing his own eyesight. For a man in his profession, if he didn't take his own life at that time, someone else was sure to do it for him. He wondered how brave he would be in that situation. Few things frightened Faulkner after all these years. In his youth it had been ignorance that kept him from feeling fear. Now it was experience. But to go blind?

"Can we talk about something else, Indian?" he asked.

"Sure, Faulkner," Tall Fellow said, "sure . . . remember that day, years ago, in Rock City? The Buckland gang . . ."

Rock City, Arkansas, 1875
The young bounty hunter and young hired killer withdrew and went back to the center of town.

"We can choose our own battleground," Tall Fellow told Faulkner as they stood in front of their hotel.

"Is that what you learned from your elders?" Faulkner asked.

"Don't scoff," Tall Fellow said. "I learned a lot sitting at the feet of those men."

"I wasn't scoffing," Faulkner said seriously. "I was just wondering."

"Oh . . . well, yeah, that's what I learned."

"Think we should bring the local law into this?" Faulkner asked.

"I don't know if we have time," Tall Fellow said. "Those fellas are going to come looking for us pretty quick."

"As long as they don't decide to run for it," Faulkner said.

"I think we tweaked Buckland's ego, don't you?" Tall Fellow asked. "He isn't going to run. He's going to want to teach us a lesson."

Faulkner decided to bow to Tall Fellow's experience in this matter. They may have been the same age, but Tall Fellow had grown up out here. That gave him the edge in decision making, as far as Faulkner was concerned.

On the other side, Henry Tall Fellow was glad that Faulkner did not feel the need to make all the decisions all the time. He hadn't liked the Easterner when they first met, but the money gun was beginning to grow on him — starting back at the moment when he'd shot the head off that pygmy rattler.

"So, where do we make our stand?" Faulkner asked.

Tall Fellow went into the hotel lobby and came out with two straight-backed wooden chairs. He set them down and turned to Faulkner.

"Right here."

Buckland came down off the boardinghouse

porch and eyed each of his men.

"I want these two jaspers dead, you got that?" he said.

They all nodded and one of them said, "We got that, boss, but . . ."

"But what?"

"What about the sheriff?"

"If he gets in the way," Buckland said, "kill him, too."

The men all liked that, and almost cheered. It wasn't often they got the okay to kill a lawman.

"But don't get yourselves distracted by a shiny little tin target," Buckland warned. "I want them two bounty hunters dead first!"

"Okay, boss."

"Let's go, then," Buckland said. "They're in town somewhere."

"What if they left town?" one of the men asked.

"With the price on my head?" Buckland asked. "They're not going anywhere. They're in town and they won't be hard to find."

CHAPTER 31

Tom Buckland's prediction was very true. Faulkner and Tall Fellow were not hard to find. They were still seated in front of the hotel when they spotted Buckland and his boys coming down the street and were, in turn, spotted.

"Here they come," Tall Fellow said.

"A lot of them," Faulkner said.

"We knew that."

"Well," Faulkner said, "there are two fewer then there might have been."

They both stood up.

"I'll take across the street," Tall Fellow said.

"Two against nine?" Faulkner asked. "Are we ready for that?"

"I don't know," Tall Fellow said. "Are we?"

"I guess we're about to find out."

Tall Fellow nodded, stepped off the boardwalk and walked across the street.

Faulkner stepped down into the street and

161

waited.

Buckland saw one man moving across the street and the other standing just in front of the hotel.

"Hobbs," Buckland said, "take three men and kill the one across the street. The rest of you are with me. We're takin' that one." He pointed.

They all drew their guns and quickened their pace.

Faulkner saw that Buckland was in the group of men moving toward him.

"Lucky me," he said to himself. "I'm going to get to collect my fee."

He started toward the men.

The streets were empty. Word got around fast when something like this was going to happen.

Get off the streets.

Get behind locked doors.

But watch from your window.

And if the word had gotten to the sheriff, he was staying inside, just like everyone else.

As Buckland and his men got closer, Faulkner wasted no time. He drew his gun and fired.

■ ■ ■ ■

As Faulkner fired, Tall Fellow drew and did the same. Neither man was able to take a look at the other. Each was on his own.

CHAPTER 32

1898

"There it is," Faulkner said.

"Gunman's Crossing," Tall Fellow said, shaking his head. "It does exist."

"A town with no law," Faulkner said. "You'd think it would be in a state of perpetual chaos."

"Maybe it is," Tall Fellow said. "We just can't hear it from here. Let's get a little closer."

"Hang on a minute," Faulkner said, putting out a hand to stop his friend. "Let's not be in such a hurry."

"What's on your mind?"

"There's a chance one or both of us might be recognized in that town. We've put away a lot of men, some of whom might have gotten out and come here."

"I've put away a lot of men," Tall Fellow corrected him. "You've put a lot of men in the ground."

"Whatever," Faulkner said. "The point is, we ride in there together and we're going to attract attention."

"You've got a point," Tall Fellow admitted. "Okay, I'll ride in first, you follow me in a few hours."

"I was thinking more like a day apart," Faulkner said, "just to be sure."

"Okay, then you follow me first thing tomorrow morning."

"No, I was thinking you'd follow me first thing in the morning."

"Why should you go first?"

"Because if you go first you're liable to get killed before I get there."

"Are you saying I don't know how to do my job?" Tall Fellow demanded.

"I'm saying you've been making some bad decisions lately. Like in Denver — and by the way, you still haven't paid me back for bailing you out."

"Don't worry," Tall Fellow said. "You'll get your money."

"I don't want my money," Faulkner said. "I want to go into town first. You let me do that and I'll call that debt square."

Tall Fellow stared at his friend for a few moments.

"You're not going to do anything until I get there?" he asked finally.

"Just scout the place out, make sure Sunday is there," Faulkner said.

"You won't try to take him to complete your own job?"

"I won't fire a shot until you get there. I'm not out to steal your bounty, Tall Fellow. Don't tell me that after all these years I still have to convince you of that fact?"

"No," Tall Fellow said. "No, you don't. I'm sorry, Faulkner. Like you said, I've been making some bad decisions lately. And you're right, I'd probably ride on down there, have a few drinks and go after the whole gang alone. I hate this damned Indian blood!"

"You liar. You're proud of your Indian blood. You're just saying what you think I want to hear."

"Fine," Tall Fellow said. "You go first. I'll ride in tomorrow and we'll find each other. You can tell me what you found out, if he's there or not."

"He's there," Faulkner said, "with his whole gang and the money they stole from that bank. I think we both know that."

"Well, get going, before I change my mind," Tall Fellow said. "I'll make a cold camp and follow you tomorrow."

He put out his hand and they shook.

"Good luck," Tall Fellow said. "I think

you'll need it to stay alive in that town until I can get there and save your ass — again!"

There were three hotels in Gunman's Crossing, two rooming houses, five saloons, and three whorehouses. Jack Sunday picked out one of the hotels for himself, then told all his men to find someplace else to stay.

"I don't want any of you around me while we're here," he told them.

Hobbs looked hurt and said, "We can't even have a drink together?"

"What did I say, Hobbs?"

"Okay, okay," Hobbs said. "We'll all stay away from you while we're here. Is it okay if we have a drink with each other?"

"Hobbs, I don't care if you fuck each other," Sunday said, "Just stay . . . away . . . from . . . me."

Sunday went into his hotel, leaving his men standing outside.

"Whataya think that's about?" one of the men asked Hobbs.

"How the fuck should I know?" Hobbs asked. "Ya know what? Stay away from me, too!"

CHAPTER 33

Faulkner rode into Gunman's Crossing the way he rode into any town. He was usually looking for somebody, so it didn't take much acting.

But he wasn't going to go looking for anybody just yet. The normal thing to do would be to put his horse up at the livery and find himself a hotel room. He ignored the looks he got from men on the street, figuring they all had prices on their heads. There were no women in sight on the street.

At the livery he handed his horse over to a shifty-looking gent who made him pay two dollars first.

"That horse better be here when I come for him," Faulkner said, "or I'll shove that two dollars up your ass. You got that?"

The man tried to match stares with Faulkner, but finally had to look away.

"Yeah, sure, I got it."

Faulkner figured this was the best way to

act in this town. He didn't want to get tabbed as a soft guy. Better to be known as a hard man.

He left the livery, carrying his rifle and saddlebags. On his way to a hotel he ignored stares from men he passed on the street. He figured he'd first have to stand up to their stares before any of them actually stepped up to try to intimidate him. That would come later, and he'd be ready. He was sure that every man in that town was on the run, or had a price on his head. If he had to kill any to make his point, he wouldn't lose any sleep over it.

He really didn't have any fear of being recognized. He had never worn a badge in his life, and his reputation as a money gun certainly entitled him to be in a place like Gunman's Crossing, since popular opinion of such a man usually lumped him in with outlaws, thieves and indiscriminate killers.

On the other hand, while lawmen lumped bounty hunters in with killers, killers lumped bounty men in with lawman. If Tall Fellow was recognized, someone might try to kill him. It was for that reason Faulkner did not want his friend riding into town first, and not that he was afraid Tall Fellow would get drunk and make a mistake.

Although that was certainly a possibility

in Tall Fellow's present state.

Faulkner stopped in the first hotel he came to. It really didn't matter to him where he stayed, so the state of the accommodations didn't concern him. It suited him that the building was standing.

"Got a room?" he asked the clerk.

"Who wants ta know?" the tall, skinny clerk asked.

"I do," Faulkner said. "I'm tired and in no mood for games. If you don't want my money, say so. I'll be on my way. If you just want to give me a hard time I'll just put a bullet in you, and still be on my way."

"Okay, okay," the man said. "Don't get offended." He opened the register book and said, "Sign in."

"You're kidding, right?"

The man withdrew the book, turned, picked a key off the wall and handed it to Faulkner.

"Room seven, upstairs," he said. "Enjoy your stay."

Faulkner took the key and, without another word, went up the stairs.

Outside of town Tall Fellow made his cold camp and chewed on some tough beef jerky. He hated like hell to admit that Faulkner was right. He probably would have gotten himself killed if he'd gone into town on his own. Maybe he'd been trying to do that ever since the doctor had told him about his failing eyesight.

He walked to his saddlebags, reached in and touched the bottle of whiskey he had there. Touched the smooth surface of the bottle, but finally left it where it was. Instead, he grabbed his canteen and washed the tough, dry meat down with a swig of water.

He sat down with his back up against his saddle. It wasn't even dark yet. Sitting here doing nothing, waiting for morning, was going to be tough. He was not the kind of man who did well sitting or standing still. Maybe there was some way he could sneak into town without being seen.

He thought about the whiskey bottle in his saddlebags, then shook his head and tried to think about something else. There was something about the Jack Sunday gang that Faulkner didn't know. He wondered what his friend would say when he finally told him what that was.

He sat and stared straight ahead, his mind drifting back almost twenty-five years, as it had been doing a lot lately. . . .

CHAPTER 34

Rock City, 1875

During the relatively short time he'd been in the West, Faulkner had not been involved in many shootouts of this kind. Mostly he'd killed men one on one, usually facing them to give them an equal break — even when they didn't deserve one.

There was nothing equal about this situation. Of the nine men approaching them, five were heading for him, while four made their way toward Tall Fellow. Faulkner, still with something of the Easterner in him, marveled at how they would simply come walking up the street toward him.

His first shot struck one man in the chest, spinning him and dumping him onto the ground. The others began firing back at him and he had to dive for cover as lead zipped over his head. He heard it strike the front of the hotel, shattering glass.

From behind a horse trough, he fired

several times, hoping to hit Buckland with at least one of those shots. He saw another man stagger and fall, but Buckland himself had broken off and gone for cover.

Suddenly, the shooting stopped, even from across the street. Everybody had to be reloading and he took the opportunity to do the same.

Across the street Tall Fellow had held his own in the first volley, putting two men down before he was also forced to reload. Both he and Faulkner had decided not to use their rifles. They realized they were much better shots with their pistols.

Tall Fellow had taken cover behind a couple of barrels, and as he reloaded he realized there was no shooting anymore, not even from across the street. He hoped Faulkner had been able to avoid getting killed, because if he was alone, he was in a lot of trouble.

Buckland thought the two bounty hunters were crazy. Faced with nine armed men, most men would have broken and ran. Not these two. They stood their ground and only went for cover when they had to.

Buckland reloaded, then looked over at the two men he had left on his side of the street. They had all taken cover behind a buckboard.

"Pin him down," he told them. "I'm going around behind the hotel. I'm gonna come at him from the lobby."

The two men waved, then started shooting. Buckland ran down a nearby alley.

Across the street Tall Fellow raised his head and drew fire, thus locating the three men who were trying to kill him. He knew that if they all just remained where they were, this could go on all day. Most likely they'd try to close in on him, so he decided to try to change his position.

On his side of the street were several businesses, all of which had closed their doors just before the shooting started. It didn't much matter, though, because all the lead flying about had taken care of most of the glass in their windows. Tall Fellow chose one of those windows and decided it was his goal.

He raised his gun, fired twice and then started running for the window. He heard the shooting behind him, felt hot lead whizzing by him like angry bees, and then leaped. . . .

Faulkner watched Tall Fellow jump through

the broken window of the hardware store. It was a good move, to get off the street. It was probably something he should do himself, as soon as Buckland and his men stopped to reload again. Luckily, they weren't smart enough to stagger their shots, so that one could reload while the others continued to fire.

He sat on his butt with his back to the trough, waiting for the shooting to stop, then realized that they were shooting without any hope of hitting him. It dawned on him that they were just trying to pin him down. The only reason for that was that somebody was trying to flank him, or trying to get around behind him.

It would be a good idea if he changed position, as Tall Fellow had done.

The question was, where to go?

Buckland made his way to the back of the hotel. He found the rear door locked, but it could not stand against him. He kicked it open and went inside, moving down a hallway that took him to a curtained doorway. As he rushed through it, he found himself behind the desk.

The clerk turned, saw him and said, "What the hell —" but never finished. Buckland clubbed him to the floor, then came around the desk and headed for the door.

Tall Fellow went through the window and just kept on going. He went through a door in the back and found himself in a storeroom. There were tools all around him — picks, shovels, axes. He grabbed an axe that reminded him of a tomahawk his father once had, and shoved the handle into his trousers. He didn't know if the outlaws would pursue him into the hardware store or not. If he knew, he could wait for them, but he would rather be on the move. Staying still was not easy for him.

There was no back door, but there was a rear window. He moved to it and peered out to see if anyone was waiting for him. He could still hear shooting from out front. Could it be possible they hadn't see him run through that window? That they thought they had him pinned down?

He picked up a wooden stool from nearby, used it to knocked the glass out of the back window, and climbed out.

CHAPTER 35

Faulkner had an idea. It was daring, but he didn't think the outlaws would believe it. He couldn't stay where he was, not if someone was working his way to him from behind. Once he got into a crossfire, he was as good as dead.

He needed to wait until they were reloading. When the last shot came, even before the echo faded, he was on his feet and running . . . toward them!

The two outlaws began to reload, quickly ejecting their spent shells and thumbing in the live ones. Once they were loaded they stood up, prepared to fire again, but what they saw stunned both of them. The bounty hunter was running at them, was almost on their position, and started to fire.

Tom Buckland came running out the front door of the hotel, expecting to see Faulkner's back as a nice big target. Instead, he saw the man running away from him, toward his two men, who were standing there, gaping. As Buckland watched, the man gunned down his two men. Buckland stole a look across the street, saw the rest of his men rushing through a window to the hardware store. He didn't know what the dumb bastards were doing, but that left him and the one bounty hunter on the street.

He stepped down off the boardwalk.

Faulkner came around the buckboard and checked the two fallen men. They were dead. He hoped they had a nice-sized bounty between them for Tall Fellow to collect.

He turned to see a lone man coming toward him from the direction of the hotel.

Tom Buckland.

Faulkner stepped out from behind the buckboard.

Tall Fellow was going out the back window when he heard them coming in the front. He stopped, climbed back in and waited, his gun in his hand. As they came rushing through the door into the storeroom, he opened fire. His first volley caught one of them in the chest, knocking him to the floor.

As he fired at the second man his gun suddenly jammed.

"Oops," the outlaw said, grinning. He raised his gun slowly and pointed it at Tall Fellow, who quickly drew the small hand axe from his belt and threw it.

Faulkner and Buckland moved toward each other.

"What's your name, kid?" Buckland asked.

"Faulkner."

"Bounty hunter?"

"No."

"Then what are you doin' here?"

"I came to kill you."

"Why? What did I ever do to you?"

"Nothing," Faulkner said. "Until I took this job I never heard of you."

"What job?"

"I told you," Faulkner said. "I'm here to kill you."

Suddenly, Buckland started to laugh.

"You're for hire?" he asked, laughing harder. "A hired killer?"

"There are lots of names for what I am, I guess."

"And your friend?"

"He's not my friend," Faulkner said, "but he is a bounty hunter. I'll kill you, and he'll collect the bounty."

"And you'll get paid."

"Yes."

"By whom?"

Faulkner shook his head.

"You get to know that someone hired me to kill you," Faulkner said. "You don't get to know who. Just know that someone hates you enough to want you dead."

"All right, then, Money Gun," Buckland said, holstering his gun, "let's see who the better man is, you or me."

"I'd rather see who the smarter man is," Faulkner said.

He didn't holster his gun, as Buckland expected him to do. Instead, he raised it and shot the man in the chest.

Tall Fellow came out of the hardware store in time to watch the confrontation between Buckland and Faulkner. He, too, expected Faulkner to holster his gun and engage in a fair fight. He was shocked when Faulkner simply shot the man dead.

By the time he reached them Faulkner was standing over the dead Buckland.

"You can collect your bounty now, Tall Fellow."

"You just shot him," the bounty hunter said.

Faulkner looked at him.

"That's my job."

"But . . . he was willing to fight it out with you fair."

Faulkner ejected the spent shell from his gun, replaced it with a live one, and then holstered the gun.

"I didn't grow up here, Tall Fellow," he said. "I don't have to follow your ridiculous code of the West. It was my job to kill him and he made it easy."

"So any way you can get it done is good?"

"You got it."

Tall Fellow looked around him at the bodies in the street.

"Is this all of them?" Faulkner asked.

"Two more in that hardware store."

"Bounties are all yours," Faulkner said.

"You leaving town?"

"My job's done. I'm going right to the livery to get on my horse and ride out. Got a job in Denver."

"Sure you don't want a share of the bounty on the rest of these fellas?" Tall Fellow asked. "You earned it."

"All yours, Tall Fellow."

He walked away.

"See you somewhere down the trail."

Faulkner waved without looking back.

CHAPTER 36

1898

Jack Sunday picked the Lucky Ace Saloon to spend his time in. If any of the other men showed up, he chased them out. The Ace was now his place.

He also chose the restaurant right across from his hotel to eat all his meals. He had steak for every meal when he could get it.

Faulkner didn't know about the steak. He only knew which saloon and which restaurant Sunday was patronizing. It had been easy to find Sunday, since they were staying at the same hotel.

Faulkner had been standing out in front of the hotel, pondering his next move, when Jack Sunday came walking out. Question answered. He didn't look at the man, but when Sunday started walking, so did Faulkner.

By late afternoon, Sunday had eaten twice at the small restaurant and stopped into the

Lucky Ace three times. He had not yet stopped at any of the whorehouses.

Also, he was obviously staying away from the other members of his gang, since he'd chased several of them out of the Ace.

Since Faulkner did not want Sunday to catch on to him, he chose a different saloon and a different restaurant. He decided to go ahead and remain in the same hotel.

Later that evening, Faulkner — satisfied that Sunday would be at the Lucky Ace for a while — went to the Happy Thief Saloon. He liked the name. It was obviously somebody's idea of irony. That required a brain. Somebody in Gunman's Crossing was more than a mindless thief and murderer.

He stood at the bar in the Thief and nursed a beer. He just had to kill time until Tall Fellow rode into town the next morning, and then they'd have to figure out how they were going to take Sunday. Sunday staying away from his own gang members might even make it easy. The gang leader obviously felt safe enough in Gunman's Crossing to not have to keep his gang around him. Still, they were in town, so when Faulkner and Tall Fellow made their move against him, they still might have to deal with the rest of the gang.

An argument broke out at a corner table

and Faulkner turned to look. There was a poker game going on. Two of the players were members of Sunday's gang. They were two of the four he had identified by watching Sunday.

They were apparently being accused of working together to take money from the other three men. Faulkner watched with interest. If the argument escalated into violence and they got themselves killed, Sunday would have two fewer men. He stood there, rooting for guns to be drawn, but it didn't happen. Instead, Sunday's two men stormed out of the place without their money.

Faulkner turned back to the bar and ordered another beer. He was still nursing that one when a woman sidled up next to him. She stood there a few moments before he turned his head and looked at her. Definitely not a saloon girl. And she wasn't drinking. There was only one other explanation. He looked straight ahead again.

"You own this place?" he asked.

"Good guess."

She was blond, about thirty-five, attractive but not beautiful. There was a confidence about her, though, that made her striking. She attracted attention, and she was standing next to him, which meant he'd attract attention.

"You're new in town," she said.

"Good guess on your part. Can I help you with something?"

"You can if you are who I think you are."

"And who do you think I am?"

"A man who hires out his gun."

"Just any man who hires out his gun?" he asked. "That would be an amazingly good guess."

"Faulkner," she said. "Your name is Faulkner."

He looked at her.

"We can talk in my office."

CHAPTER 37

They went into a small office and she seated herself behind a small, pitted desk.

"What can I do for you, Miss . . ."

"My name is Gena Miller," she said. "Mrs. I'm a widow."

"Sorry to hear it."

"Don't be. My husband was a sonofabitch. When he died two years ago, it was the best thing that ever happened to me."

"Okay. What can I do for you, Mrs. Miller?"

"You can do what you do best."

"What I do best is kill people," Faulkner said. "Just so there's no mistake."

"Oh, I understand," she said. "I am the only woman in Gunman's Crossing who owns a business. Do you know what that means?"

"That you inherited it from your husband when he died?"

"That I got it from my husband after I

killed him," she said.

"That was what I assumed you meant when you said he died."

"You're a smart man," she said. "What's a smart man like you doing in Gunman's Crossing?"

"I came across it by mistake," he said. "I never really believed it existed, so I decided to have a look."

"What do you think?"

"I like your place."

"Seems to me a man like you would find more enjoyment at the Lucky Ace. Gambling girls . . ."

"Excuse me, Mrs. Miller, but you don't know what kind of man I am."

"You're undoubtedly right," she said. "I apologize. Why don't we get back to business?"

"You wanted me to do what I do best."

"Yes," she said, "I need you to kill a man."

"Just one?"

"Yes."

"Any reason why you can't do it yourself?"

"Five."

"And what are they?"

"Five bodyguards."

"Ah. Tell me something."

"What?"

"What would you have done if you hadn't

187

seen me tonight?"

"I would have kept waiting for the right man to come through the door."

Faulkner fell silent.

"I mean, after all, you are just passing through, right?"

"That's right."

"So there's no reason you can't work for me."

"Not until I find one."

"Is that how you do business?" she asked. "You look for a reason not to do a job?"

"As a matter of fact," Faulkner said, "it is. I don't kill for no reason."

"I thought your reason would be you're being paid."

"That's what my reason would be once I take the job," he said.

"So will you take the job?"

"I need a lot more information," he said.

"Perhaps I can give you that information over a meal?" she asked.

"That sounds like a good idea," he said. "I could use a good meal."

"Good." She stood up. "I have a nice dining room upstairs, and a good cook in my employ. Why don't you wait at the bar until I get things ready?"

"All right."

She walked to the door and opened it.

"I won't be long. Steak all right?"

"Steak will be fine."

He left the office and went back to the bar.

"She make you a good offer?" the bartender asked, as he set a beer in front of Faulkner.

"I'm sorry?"

"Did she make you a good offer for your gun?"

"What makes you think she tried to buy my gun?" Faulkner asked.

"She's been waitin' for the right man for months," the bartender said. He was in his forties, very fit, with short dark hair and a well-cared-for mustache.

"And what makes you think it's me?"

The man smiled.

"Because I'm the one who told her you were here."

CHAPTER 38

The bartender's name was Zack Lawrence.

"I saw you kill a man in Abilene a few years back," he said. "I recognized you as soon as you walked in, knew you were the man she's been lookin' for."

Faulkner studied the man for a moment.

"You're in love with her."

"That doesn't matter."

"Why don't you do what she wants done?" Faulkner asked.

"I'm no gunman," Zack said. "I'm just a bartender."

"So who does she want killed?"

"That's for her to tell you."

Faulkner looked around.

"Does everyone here know who I am now?"

"No," Zack said, "not unless they recognized you on their own. But would it matter? You're safe here. As far as I know, you've never worn a badge in your life."

"No, I haven't."

"Lawmen, or ex-lawmen, or even ex-bounty hunters, they'd have a problem here. Not you. After all, you've probably killed more men than anybody else in this town."

"You're probably right."

"So have you accepted her offer?"

"I haven't heard the whole offer yet," Faulkner said. "She's going to make it over a steak."

"Ah . . ."

"Tell me about her husband."

"Thornton Miller."

Faulkner's eyebrows went up.

"Yep, that Thornton Miller."

"There's only one that I know of. I didn't make the connection."

"No reason you would. Miller is a common name."

"What happened to Miller?"

"He came here, started this place. He had put his guns down, thinking he'd be safe here."

"And he wasn't."

"Somebody shot him in the back."

"Any idea who?"

"Nobody cares," Zack said. "There's no law here. So Gena took over the place. She's the only woman running a business in town, except for two of the whorehouses."

"Two?"

"One of them is owned and run by a man."

"Seems to me the kind of men who live here," Faulkner said, "wouldn't take kindly to having a woman own a business. I mean, a real business, not a whorehouse."

"You've got that right. Whoever she wants you to kill, she wants you to do it before they kill her."

"But you won't tell me that."

"No," he said, shaking his head. "That's up to her."

"Okay," Faulkner said. "So I guess I'll just have another beer."

"Comin' up."

Faulkner was still working on that beer when Zack came over and said, "Stairway in the back. Takes you right up to the dining room."

"Should I take my beer?"

"Naw, that's okay," Zack said. "You'll have a fresh one up there."

Faulkner looked at the stairway in the back, and then back at Zack.

"Oh, don't worry," Zack said. "There's nobody up there but her."

Faulkner hesitated.

"I know you've been shot at a lot of

times," the bartender said, "but it ain't gonna happen here. She needs you."

Faulkner was thinking that this woman had shot her own husband — a one-time famed gunman — in the back. What was to stop her from doing it to him?

Well, for one thing, there was no apparent reason for her to do that.

And he did really want a steak.

"Okay," he said.

He walked to the back of the room and up the stairway. The room at the top was well lit, which was encouraging. If it had been dark at the top of the stairs, he would not have gone.

When he got to the top he saw a table set up in a small dining room. Just the one table, with Gena Miller sitting at it.

"Thanks for coming," she said. "Your steak is getting cold."

"How's the steak?" she asked, fifteen minutes later.

"Excellent," he said.

"And the vegetables?"

"Very good," he assured her. "You do have a good cook working for you."

"Yes, I do. More wine?"

"Please."

The table was small enough that all she

had to do was lean over and pour.

"You're very educated," she said.

"There are different kinds of educations."

"I meant you sound college-educated."

"A long time ago," he said, "back east."

"Yes, me, too. Where?"

"Just . . . east."

She smiled and said, "Me, too."

"And your husband?"

"Oh no," she said. "Thornton was a Westerner, through and through."

He nodded.

"You know that name, don't you?" she asked. "Thornton Miller?"

"Yes, I do."

"But you weren't surprised when I said it," she commented. "Who had the big mouth? Zack?"

"Yes."

"I should fire him."

"Somehow I don't think you will."

"No," she said, "I probably couldn't run this place without him."

"Mrs. Miller —"

"Gena," she said. "Please call me Gena."

"Gena," Faulkner said, "can we get to the person you want me to kill? The one with the five bodyguards?"

"Of course," she said. "His name is Gary Blaine. He owns the Lucky Ace."

"Uh-huh."

"And a few other businesses in town."

"Including a whorehouse?"

"How did you know that?"

"Lucky guess. Is the reason you want him dead that he's your competitor?"

"No," she said. "I don't care about competition. There's plenty to go around for all of us, that's what I think."

"But he doesn't feel the same?"

"Not at all," she said. "He wants to own it all. In a town of snakes and crooks and killers, he's the worst."

"I see."

"Or he was," she added, "until you got here."

Chapter 39

"He wants me dead."

"Then why doesn't he just kill you?" Faulkner asked. "Or have you killed?"

"Even though this town is filled with killers," she said, "there aren't that many who want to kill a woman."

"Especially not Thornton Miller's widow."

"You're right. My husband had a lot of friends here," she said.

"But none who want to bother trying to find out who killed him, right?"

She sat back.

"Anyone trying to find out would be acting like a lawman," she said. "These men would rather be caught dead than act like a lawman."

"But they idolized your husband."

"Some of them did," she said. "If they found out I killed him . . ."

"They might forget you're a woman."

"Yes."

"Then why doesn't Blaine just let the word out?" Faulkner asked.

"He doesn't know," she said. "Nobody does."

"Not even Zack?"

"He suspects, but he doesn't know."

"So why did you tell me?"

"It gives you something on me," she said. "It tells you I'm serious."

"How do you know I wasn't hired to come here and kill you?"

"If that's the case I wouldn't be able to stop you. You could do it right now and you'd probably get away with it. You might have to kill Zack, too, but you'd get away."

"Well, lucky for you that's not the case, then," he said.

"So . . . will you do it?" she asked. "I mean, while you're here you might as well make some money. What's the going rate for money guns these days?"

"It goes up," he told her, "per bodyguard."

Gary Blaine walked up to Jack Sunday, who was sitting alone at a table with a bottle of whiskey.

"Mind if I join you?"

Sunday looked up at him.

"Depends on who you are."

"I own this place," Blaine said.

"And why should that mean anything to me?"

"I can arrange for everything you have in here to be free."

Sunday sat back.

"Have a seat, Mr. Blaine."

Blaine waved to a passing saloon girl and told her to bring a fresh bottle.

"I'll have to check Gary Blaine out first," Faulkner said. "I can let you know by tomorrow night."

"You're an odd sort of gun for hire, Mr. Faulkner," she said. "I thought once we agreed on the money, that would be it."

"It's not all about the money for me," he told her. "The steak helped, but there are still other considerations."

"Oh, I see," she said. "The bodyguards. You want to take a look at the setup. I can understand that."

"Good," he said. "Then I assume there's a dessert that goes with this fine meal?"

"Oh, yes," she said with a smile, "there is definitely dessert."

Chapter 40

"Let me get this straight," Jack Sunday said to Blaine. "You want me to kill a woman?"

"Yes."

"This town is full of killers."

"Not like you," Blaine said. "They have . . . scruples."

"And I don't?"

"I've followed your career, Mr. Sunday," Blaine said. "You're the man I've been waiting for."

"And why would I do this?"

"For money."

"What makes you think I need the money?"

"Everybody needs money," Gary Blaine said.

Sunday poured himself another shot of whiskey and said, "I've got money."

"Well," Blaine said, "maybe I can sweeten the pot."

"With what?"

"The woman I want killed is Thornton Miller's widow," Blaine said. "That mean anything to you?"

Sunday sat up straight.

"I'd like it better if it was Miller himself."

"Can't help you there," Blaine said. "Somebody beat you to it."

"I didn't hear."

"He was shot in the back."

"By whom?"

"Nobody knows for sure."

"But you have an idea?"

"Yeah."

Sunday waited, then said, "Her? You think she back-shot her own husband?"

"Yes."

"Why would she?"

"He hung up his guns, but not his violent nature," Blaine said.

"Huh?"

"He used to beat her up," Blaine said. "She got tired of it."

"So whoever killed him didn't claim his rep."

"Right."

Sunday thought it over.

"A man would've done it and announced it to everyone," he said.

"I agree."

"Okay, so she did it," Sunday said. "How

does that help me? I kill her, I don't get credit for him."

"Are you tired of what you've been doing, Jack?" Blaine asked.

Sunday stared at his drink.

"I been doing it for a long time."

"Gunman's Crossing would be a good place to settle down," Blaine said. "You could have the Happy Thief if you killed Gena Miller. And the money I'll pay you. And the satisfaction of knowing you killed Thornton Miller's wife — the person who killed him."

Sunday had another drink. Was he tired of doing what he'd been doing for so many years? He knew he was tired of the men he had to use, to ride with. That was why he didn't want any of them to come near him while they were here.

"I tell you what," Blaine said. "Think it over and let me know. There's no rush. Meanwhile, whatever you want here — whiskey, women, food — it's on the house. Both here and at the whorehouse I also own."

"You own a whorehouse?"

The light in Jack Sunday's eyes told Gary Blaine he may have just hit upon his real route to recruiting the man.

■ ■ ■ ■

Faulkner finished his delicious apple pie and coffee and Gena walked him down the stairs to a back door.

"I don't think anyone should see us together anymore," she said, and he agreed.

At the door she said, "Just come into the saloon tomorrow and stand at the bar if you're going to do the job."

"And if I'm not going to do the job?" he asked. "Where do I stand then?"

"No offense, Faulkner," she said, "but if you're not going to do the job, then don't even come back into my place."

"Hey —" he said as she pushed him out the door.

"In fact," she added, "don't even stay in this town."

She slammed the door and left him standing out behind the building. He found an alley and took it back to Gunman's Crossing's main street.

He didn't even know why he had entertained her offer. He wasn't in town looking for more work; he was in town to help Tall Fellow collect his bounty on Jack Sunday.

But the steak dinner had been good.

■ ■ ■ ■

Tall Fellow stared up at the sky, lying on his back next to the fire he had decided to go ahead and build. He needed the warmth, and he wasn't cooking bacon or making coffee or anything that could be smelled from miles away.

He had played back the whole Tom Buckland affair in his head over and over during this hunt for Jack Sunday. After it had all been over and Faulkner had left, he'd gone back to collect the bodies for the bounties, and one had been missing. One man had not been dead, and he had gotten away. It had taken Tall Fellow many years to find out who that man was. It was like an unfinished part of his history that he had to track down that final man. It connected his life then to his life now.

He had never, over the years, during all the times they had worked together, told Faulkner what had happened. He didn't know why. Maybe it never seemed important, but it was important to him now.

He wondered what Faulkner would think about the young man who'd been part of the Tom Buckland gang growing up to be

Jack Sunday, who now had a gang of his own.

CHAPTER 41

Faulkner went directly back to his hotel and turned in. He could have gone to the Lucky Ace to check on Jack Sunday but decided there was no need. Sunday was in town and wasn't going anywhere soon. The only reason to even come to Gunman's Crossing was to lie low for a while.

Or to kill somebody.

Tall Fellow rose in the morning, kicked dirt on the fire until it was out, then mounted up and rode into Gunman's Crossing. He was pleased to see that his arrival went without much notice. The men walking the streets didn't care who he was, unless they saw the glint of the sun on a badge.

He also breathed a sigh of relief when he came within sight of one of the hotels and saw Faulkner very casually sitting out front.

Good. He was still alive.

■ ■ ■ ■

Jack Sunday woke that morning, rolled over and looked at the girl in the bed next to him. She had looked a lot better last night when he was drunk. And, of course, when she was free.

He got out of the bed and walked to the window so he could look down at the town. What more perfect place could there be to settle down than a town with no law? The only other question he had to answer was, did he want to settle down and give up the life he was leading?

If he could put together the right gang it would be different, but they were approaching a new century, and he couldn't find dependable men anymore. It wasn't like when he started riding with Tom Buckland all those years ago. Back then every man in the gang was good — or was that like being drunk the night before when he picked out this whore? Maybe the older he got and the further away he got from those days, the better the memories became. Actually, Tom Buckland was a good leader, but he was far from perfect. He was a good planner, but he wasn't very smart.

Sunday considered himself a good planner and a smart man. He was so smart, in fact, that he couldn't stand to hold a conversation with any of his men that didn't have to do with robbing or killing.

So now he had an opportunity to settle down, have his own place in Gunman's Crossing, with no law to bother him, and he'd only have to talk to people if he wanted to. And the price seemed small enough.

All he had to do was kill a woman he didn't know — and he'd done that enough times before.

Faulkner watched Tall Fellow ride past, on his way toward the livery. He decided to wait where he was for the bounty hunter to come back. He didn't know where Sunday was at the moment, but it was a good bet he was either still in his room or across the street at the restaurant he favored. If he wasn't in one if those locations, then it would probably be a whorehouse. From what he had learned about the town, there were three.

He thought some more about the previous night's offer from the widow of Thornton Miller. Miller was about ten years older than Faulkner — or he would have been if he were still alive. When Faulkner first came west, Miller already had a reputation as a gunman. It had been so many years since he'd heard anything new about him, though, that he'd just assumed the man was dead. Well, he was dead, but only two years in the ground. Faulkner would have liked to meet Miller, but that wasn't possible. But he had been given the chance to help the man's widow. And where was the harm in picking up some money once he was finished with his favor for Tall Fellow?

It took fifteen minutes for Tall Fellow to come walking back up the street, carrying his saddlebags and rifle. It would make sense for him to stop, since this was the first hotel he'd come to.

Faulkner deliberately did not look at his friend as he mounted the boardwalk.

"Excuse me," Tall Fellow said.

Faulkner looked up.

"You staying in this hotel?"

"I am."

"Is it any good?"

"Beds are better than the ground."

"Sounds good to me."

"The clerk's probably going to ask you to sign the register."

"Thanks for the warning."

Tall Fellow went inside to get a room, and Faulkner remained where he was.

Another fifteen minutes later Tall Fellow

came out, stopped, and made a production out of rolling a cigarette.

"Where is Sunday?" he asked, without looking at Faulkner.

"He's actually staying in this hotel," Faulkner said. "He's either inside or in that restaurant across the street." He also told him about the likelihood that Sunday might be in a whorehouse if he wasn't in one of those places.

"The only other place he favors is the Lucky Ace saloon."

"And do you favor that saloon?"

"I do my drinking at the Happy Thief."

"And his men?"

"All over town, but they apparently have orders to stay away from him."

"That's good for us."

"Saloons aren't open yet," Faulkner said. "Get yourself something to eat across the street."

"Where are you going to be?"

"Right here."

"See you in a while."

Tall Fellow stepped down and Faulkner watched him walk across the street and enter the restaurant. Suddenly he realized he was hungry. Should have told Tall Fellow he'd be going to get something to eat himself. Now he'd have to sit until Tall Fellow was finished. It was just as well. Tall Fellow had spent the night on the ground in a cold camp. It was only fair.

CHAPTER 42

Sunday left the whorehouse and headed back toward his hotel, then crossed the street and entered the restaurant. He'd seen the man seated in front of the hotel, but didn't give him any more thought than he gave the other diners around him. He grabbed a table in the back and called the waiter over.

"Steak and eggs, sir?"

"And coffee."

"Comin' up."

Sunday was going to eat a leisurely breakfast, and by the time he was done he was going to come to a decision about whether or not to kill the woman for Gary Blaine. However, if he was going to do it, Blaine was going to have to understand that Jack Sunday didn't work for anybody. If he did it, he intended to come out the other end as Blaine's partner — whether the man liked it or not.

When Faulkner saw Sunday coming down the street he remained still. He couldn't afford to give any indication that he recognized him, or that his appearance meant anything to him. If Sunday entered the hotel he'd keep his eyes straight ahead, as he had with Tall Fellow. Instead, Sunday headed across the street to the restaurant and went inside.

Now it was up to Tall Fellow to maintain his composure with his meal ticket right in front of him.

As Jack Sunday entered, Tall Fellow recognized him, not only from his posters, but from almost twenty-five years ago. He was bigger, heavier, older, but Tall Fellow could still see the young man he had shot all that time ago.

Too bad he had not shot him twice.

When Sunday's steak came, he took a bite and his eyes moved around the room until they came to a stop on one man. As he chewed he tried to place him. He couldn't, and it bothered him. He knew him from somewhere. It would come to him, eventually.

■ ■ ■ ■

When Jack Sunday's eyes came to a stop on him, Tall Fellow could almost physically feel them. He was eating steak and eggs of his own, and kept his head down and his eyes on his plate. He was tempted to try to take Sunday then and there, but there were too many other people in the place — most of them wearing guns. Besides, he and Faulkner had each agreed not to try to take the man alone.

He kept eating his breakfast, wondering — if Sunday had not already recognized him — how long it would take him to do so.

Tall Fellow finished eating first, paid his bill and walked out. He didn't look in Sunday's direction at all, but felt the man's eyes on him every step of the way.

He crossed over to the hotel, stepped up on the walk and stopped.

"We need to talk."

"The Happy Thief, as soon as it opens."

Tall Fellow went inside. Faulkner stood up and went in search of his own breakfast.

Jack Sunday watched the man walk out of

the restaurant, even more convinced that he knew him. And it was more than just having seen a poster, or maybe being in the same jail cell some time.

This was a face from his past, and he was going to place it before the day was out.

Tall Fellow was already at the bar when Faulkner walked into the Happy Thief. He joined him there, but left some room between them.

The bartender was not Zack, and Faulkner didn't know him, so he just ordered a beer without any other comments. He was just hoping that Gena would not put in an appearance. He wasn't ready with an answer for her yet.

As the bartender moved away Faulkner looked around and saw that he and Tall Fellow were the first two customers, so he moved closer so they could talk.

"He recognized me," Tall Fellow said.

"What? What are you talking about?"

"There's something I didn't tell you."

"About what?"

"Jack Sunday. We've met before."

"You and him?"

"All three of us."

"What the hell are you talking about, Indian?" Faulkner demanded.

"The Buckland gang," Tall Fellow said. "All those years ago? We got them all but one."

"One?"

"Sunday," Tall Fellow said. "He got away. I put a bullet in him, but he got away."

"You never told me one got away."

Tall Fellow shrugged.

"Didn't seem important."

"And you're choosing to tell me now?"

"There's no danger of him knowing you," Tall Fellow said. "You and him never came face to face back then."

"So how do you know he recognized you?"

"I could feel it. I don't think he placed me, but he knows he's seen me before."

"We may have to move fast, then, before he does place you," Faulkner said. "He's keeping away from his men. Doesn't seem to want to socialize with them."

"So maybe we can take him in the Lucky Ace?" Tall Fellow asked. "If he's on his own. Is there anybody else likely to take a hand?"

"Doesn't seem so," Faulkner said. "I think everybody here fights their own battles."

"Is there any bad news?"

"Maybe. I got a job offer."

"What? I think I need to hear about this."

"I'll tell you." He gave Tall Fellow the story of Thornton Miller's widow and her problem. And their problem.

"Since this fella Blaine has a bunch of bodyguards, the Lucky Ace may not be the place to take Sunday."

"So we can figure out a better place," Tall Fellow said. "For now, tell me . . . you going to take this job?"

Chapter 43

"You're getting your money," Faulkner said to Tall Fellow. "Why shouldn't I get mine?"

"I told you I'd share the bounty with you."

"No," Faulkner said, "I don't want your money. I want my own."

"So you're going to go up against these five bodyguards to kill this man? Has this woman got a hold over you already?"

"It's not the woman, Tall Fellow," Faulkner said.

"Ah," Tall Fellow said, "it's the legend. The Thornton legend."

"Look, I haven't made my mind up yet," Faulkner said. "I may not do it. I'll check the guy out today and make up my mind."

"Okay," Tall Fellow said.

"Okay what?"

"Okay, you came all this way to help me out," the bounty hunter said. "If you decide to take that job, I'll back you."

"I'm not asking you to do that."

"I know it," Tall Fellow said. "I'm offering. After all, if I let you go against five bodyguards alone, I'll probably never hear the end of it."

"What makes you think I'd come out of that alive?" Faulkner asked.

"Are you kidding?" Tall Fellow asked. "They would be outnumbered."

The batwing doors opened and several men came walking in.

"We have to get out of here before we attract attention," Faulkner said. "And I don't want to run into Gena Miller yet."

They turned and headed for the door.

"Want to walk out separately?" Faulkner asked.

"What the hell," Tall Fellow said. "If anybody wants to come after us, let them come."

They walked through the batwing doors together.

Jack Sunday walked into the Lucky Ace and went right to the bar.

"Tell your boss I'm here."

The bartender stared into Sunday's eyes and decided not to tell him he didn't know who he was. He'd just tell his boss "some guy" wanted to see him.

"Sure thing."

The barman left the bar and walked to the office in the back, went inside. Moments later Gary Blaine came out with him.

"Eddie," he said to the bartender as they reached the bar, "get me and my friend a beer, will you?"

"Sure thing, boss."

"Good morning, Jack."

"I made up my mind," Sunday said.

"Good," Blaine said. "I was hoping it wouldn't take you long."

As Eddie put two beers on the bar, Blaine picked one up and handed it to Jack Sunday, then picked the other one up for himself.

"Let's drink to it."

"Not so fast," Sunday said. "We still got some negotiatin' to do."

"Fine," Blaine said. "We can do that over a beer, can't we?"

Sunday stared at Blaine for a few moments, then said, "Why?" and drank his beer down, spilling much of it over his chin and onto his chest.

CHAPTER 44

Faulkner took Tall Fellow over to the Lucky Ace and they peered in one of the front windows.

"Who's that sitting with Sunday?" Tall Fellow asked. "He's too well-dressed to be one of his men."

"I'm pretty sure that's Gary Blaine."

"The man you're supposed to kill?"

"That's right."

Tall Fellow looked at Faulkner.

"They're just sitting there, Faulkner, waiting for us."

Faulkner kept looking through the window, moving his gaze around the room.

"We can just walk in and take them," Tall Fellow said.

"No," Faulkner said.

"Why not?"

"Gena said he has five bodyguards." Faulkner looked at Tall Fellow. "Where are they?"

"Maybe she was lying to you," Tall Fellow suggested.

"Why? To make the job sound harder so I wouldn't take it?"

"Doesn't make sense."

"No, it doesn't." Faulkner looked around. "Let's get away from here before we're spotted. We'll have to figure this out."

Blaine and Sunday had taken their drinks — a second beer for Sunday — to a back table, where Sunday laid it out for the other man.

Blaine started to laugh.

"What's so funny?"

"You want to be my partner?" Blaine asked.

"That's right."

"I'm not looking for a partner, Mr. Sunday," Blaine said. "I'm looking for an employee."

"I'm not anybody's employee," Sunday said. "You want that woman dead, it's gonna be on my terms. Otherwise, I can just go about my business."

"I offered you money and her business," Blaine said. "That's not good enough for you?"

"I got money," Sunday said. "And I ain't interested in owning a saloon."

Blaine had a feeling.

"What kind of business would you like to own?"

Sunday smiled.

"Now we're negotiatin'."

As Faulkner and Tall Fellow turned to leave the saloon, two men stepped out of the alley next to it, their guns in their hands and pointed at them.

"Can we help you fellas?" one of them asked.

"Actually," Faulkner said, "we've been drinking over at the Happy Thief and were wondering if we should change to the Lucky Ace."

"Any suggestions?" Tall Fellow added.

"Yep," the other man said, "I got a suggestion. Stand still and don't move while my partner relieves you of your guns."

"Now why would we want to do that?" Faulkner asked. "And why would you want our guns?"

"Because we got our guns out, and you don't," the first man said.

"You try to take my gun," Faulkner said, "and we're really going to answer a question I've been asking myself for a long time."

"Oh yeah?" the second man asked. "What question's that?"

"Whether or not I can successfully draw against an already drawn gun," Faulkner said. "What do you think, Tall Fellow?"

"I'd put my money on you, Faulkner."

Now, they didn't expect the two men to recognize Tall Fellow's name, but were hoping that Faulkner's name would ring a bell — and, apparently, it did.

"You're Faulkner?" the second man asked.

"That's right."

"Listen," the second man said, "our boss owns this place. I think he'd like to buy you a drink."

"You think so?" Faulkner asked. "What about my friend here?"

"We don't know him," the first man said.

"He can go," the second one added.

"The first thing that has to go is your guns," Faulkner said. "Why don't you boys just put them up? We don't want anybody getting hurt . . . accidentally, do we?"

The two men exchanged a glance, then shrugged and holstered their guns.

"You going inside for a drink?" Tall Fellow asked.

"Why not?" Faulkner asked. "A free drink's a free drink, right?"

Tall Fellow looked at the two bodyguards — both in their thirties and similarly dressed in black — and said, "I'll pass."

"You ain't invited," the first man said.

Tall Fellow stared at him.

"We'll see each other again," he told both of the men. "I don't like having a gun pulled on me for no reason."

"We had a reason," the first one said. "It's our job."

"I'll see you later, Faulkner," Tall Fellow said.

"I'll come over to the Happy Thief when I'm finished here."

"Who is that guy?" the first man asked.

"Somebody I met here in town," Faulkner said.

"I don't like him," the second man said.

"Seems like the feeling is mutual," Faulkner said. "Should we go inside? It would be rude to keep your boss waiting."

"Oh, he don't know you're comin'," the first man said. "But trust me, he's gonna want to buy you a drink."

"Like I said," Faulkner replied, "a free drink is a free drink."

CHAPTER 45

Faulkner entered the saloon ahead of the two bodyguards. He'd managed to get Tall Fellow out of harm's way, and he had a good idea of why the bodyguards thought their boss would want to buy him a drink.

As they approached the table, both Gary Blaine and Jack Sunday looked up at them, wondering why they were being interrupted.

"What's going on, boys?" Blaine asked his two men.

"This here fella was lookin' in the window, boss," the first man said. "When we braced him he said his name was Faulkner."

"We thought you might wanna talk to him," the other man said.

"The Faulkner?" Blaine asked. "The Money Gun?"

"I'm the only Faulkner I know of."

"Faulkner," the man said, "my name's Gary Blaine. This is my . . . associate, Jack Sunday."

"Can't say either name rings a bell," Faulkner said. "Sorry."

"No reason why mine should," Blaine said.

Sunday scowled at Faulkner.

"What's a hired gun doin' in Gunman's Crossing?" he asked.

"The name of the town just had a certain ring to it," Faulkner said. "Thought I'd check it out."

"You wanted anywhere?" Sunday asked.

"Not that I know of."

"Most of the men in this town are," the outlaw said.

Faulkner looked at Sunday and said, "I'll bet that makes their mothers very proud."

Blaine started to laugh. Sunday didn't think it was so funny, and he started to get up.

"You know, Jack," Blaine said, "I think we can finish our business a little later. I really think Mr. Faulkner and I should have a talk."

Sunday looked at Blaine, then at Faulkner. This was Faulkner's first close-up look at Sunday. He and Blaine obviously came from two ends of the spectrum. Although they were about the same age — mid-forties, which made them contemporaries of Faulkner — Blaine was well-dressed and obviously educated, while Jack Sunday was obviously uneducated, and barely civilized.

"Got no use for a hired gun, anyway," he said. "I'm gonna get some fresh air."

"You do that, Jack."

Sunday gave Faulkner another hard stare, then left the saloon.

"Why don't you boys stand by the bar," Blaine said to his bodyguards. "Have a drink."

"Sure, boss."

"Have a seat, Mr. Faulkner," Blaine invited. "Can I get you a drink?"

"A beer would be fine."

He made a signal to the bartender, who brought over one beer. The man was obviously well trained. Faulkner had not seen anything in Blaine's signal that made him think of beer.

"You shouldn't push him, you know," Blaine said.

"Push whom?"

"Sunday."

"I wasn't aware I was."

"Saying you didn't recognize his name," Blaine said. "He thinks he's left quite a mark on the West."

"Sorry to disappoint him," Faulkner said.

"You honestly don't know who he is?"

"I'm not a bounty hunter."

"No," Blaine said, "of course not. Your profession is much more . . . precise than that."

"Your boys said you might want to buy me a drink," Faulkner said. "What would the reason for that be?"

"First, why were you lookin' in my window?" Blaine asked.

"Trying to figure out if I should drink here instead of the Happy Thief."

"Well, the answer to that is very simple," Blaine said. "Have you been to the Thief?"

"Yes," Faulkner said.

"And?"

"I have to admit your beer is better."

"Everything is better over here, Mr. Faulkner."

"Just Faulkner."

"Tell me, Faulkner, have you met the owner of the Thief?"

Now here he had to decide whether or not a lie would come back to bite him.

"A woman claiming to be Thornton Miller's widow? I met her."

"Oh, she doesn't claim to be Miller's widow," Blaine said. "She is Miller's widow."

"Interesting."

"I'll tell you something else you may find interesting," Blaine said. "I've got a proposition for you."

"Let's hear it."

"First I have a question for you," Blaine said, "and I'm afraid your life may depend on the answer."

Faulkner turned his head. The two body-guards had their guns out again, as did the bartender. More signals he did not catch. Apparently, Blaine's men were a well-trained bunch.

"Looks to me like I better think over this answer very carefully."

"It's just one question," Blaine said. "The answer should be fairly simple. And I have to warn you, I'm pretty good at knowing when I'm being lied to."

"Okay, then," Faulkner said, "before my beer gets warm maybe you can ask it."

Blaine laughed.

"I like a man who gets right to the point."

"The point being?"

"Have you been hired by Gena Miller to kill me?" Gary Blaine asked.

Faulkner stared the man right in the eyes and said without hesitation, "Mr. Blaine, I can safely say that I have definitely not been hired to kill you."

CHAPTER 46

"What about Jack Sunday?"

"What about him?"

"You're not here to kill him, are you?"

"I told you," Faulkner lied. "I have no idea who he is."

Blaine leaned back in his chair and regarded Faulkner across the table.

"I could use a man like you in my operation, Faulkner," he said.

"What operation is that, Mr. Blaine?"

"Gary, please," Blaine said. "Just call me Gary. I'm talking abut this saloon and various other businesses in town."

Faulkner turned to look at the men at the bar, who still had their guns out.

"Looks to me like you've got plenty of help."

Blaine waved his hand and the men holstered their guns. The bartender stowed his behind the bar.

"I can use a good man," Blaine said.

"Somebody I can depend on."

It was Faulkner's turn to sit back. He was trying to get a look around the saloon without seeming obvious. If there were more bodyguards hidden, he wanted to find out where.

"I don't consider Gunman's Crossing an ideal spot to settle down," he said.

"Who's askin' you to settle down?" Blaine asked. "I'm only askin' you to work for me for a while."

"How long is a while?"

"Until you get tired," Blaine said. "I would pay you very well."

"I was planning on leaving tomorrow," Faulkner said.

"Why don't you think it over?" Blaine said. "Give me an answer in the morning."

"It would help if I could talk to some of your men," Faulkner said. "You know, find out what kind of boss you are?"

"It was Kirk and Ben who brought you in here," Blaine said. "Talk to them."

"That it?" Faulkner asked. "You only have two bodyguards right now?"

Blaine smiled and said, "They're the two you can talk to. Let's just leave it at that."

Men were starting to enter the saloon and belly up to the bar.

"Looks like it might start to get busy in

here," Faulkner said.

"It's busy every day," Blaine said. "Look, I'll make sure Kirk and Ben are available to you — in here, or outside. Your choice."

"I'll let you know," Faulkner said. "I'm not real impressed with them."

"Why not?"

"They had me dead to rights outside," Faulkner said, "and they let me talk them into holstering their guns."

"Maybe they were influenced by your reputation," Blaine suggested.

"Well, if I wasn't impressed with them before, that's certainly not going to do it."

Faulkner stood up, made a show of pushing in his chair, and then looked around. The Lucky Ace was certainly larger and better outfitted than the Happy Thief.

"Impressive place you have here," he said, looking around.

"I made sure it was," Blaine said. "Think over my offer, Faulkner. You know where to reach me."

Faulkner found Tall Fellow standing at the bar in the Happy Thief.

"So?"

"Behind the walls," Faulkner said. "You can barely see the cutouts in the wall, but he's got bodyguards behind the walls."

"Cutouts big enough to see through, or shoot through?"

"Both."

"So you can't take him in the saloon."

"Doubtful."

"You'll have to find out how he uses them when he leaves the saloon."

"He offered me a job, told me I could talk to two of his men — those two who drew down on us — before I make up my mind."

"Maybe you can get the information out of them, then. Just get them talking."

"That's what I was thinking," Faulkner said.

"What about Sunday?"

"He left when we started talking."

"So if we take him today, is that going to ruin your shot at this fella Blaine?"

Faulkner rubbed his jaw.

"I don't know . . . maybe we can take them both in the same day."

"How do we do that?"

"I don't know," Faulkner said. "Let's have a beer and figure it out."

CHAPTER 47

"The key may be talking to his men," Tall Fellow said over a beer. "They might say something . . . helpful."

"I don't want to interfere with you taking Sunday," Faulkner said. "I'm supposed to be helping you out with that, not making it harder."

"I'll need your help with his gang," Tall Fellow said, "if they try to get involved. If he's staying away from them, I should be able to take him alone."

"It would be good if we could both make our move at the same time."

"That only works if Sunday really is isolated from his men, and if you can do the same with Blaine and his bodyguards."

The Happy Thief was starting to do a brisk business when suddenly the door to the office opened and Gena Miller came out.

"That the boss?" Tall Fellow asked.

"That's her."

"Handsome woman."

"Got nothing to do with it."

"I was just saying."

"I'll introduce you."

Gena came over to where they were standing and smiled at Faulkner.

"Do we have to go into my office for this?" she asked.

"I don't think so," he said. "I'll take the job."

"Thank you. Did we discuss money?"

"We did not," Faulkner said.

"Are you reasonable?"

"I'm high," Faulkner said. "Very high."

"My husband left me well situated," she said. "I don't think that will be a problem."

"Gena, this is Henry Tall Fellow," Faulkner said. "If anyone asks, he and I just met today."

"But you didn't?"

"No," Faukner said. "We came here together."

"Hello, Mr. Tall Fellow."

"Ma'am."

"Are you in the same business as your friend?"

"No, ma'am," Tall Fellow said. "I'm a bounty hunter."

"And you're here working?"

"I am."

"I won't ask who it is you're hunting," she said. "It's none of my business." She switched her gaze to Faulkner. "When will you do it?"

"Soon."

"Then I suppose I should pay you?"

"Half," he said. "Half when I'm done."

"Then we do have to go to my office. Mr. Tall Fellow? Will you come with us?"

"No, ma'am," Tall Fellow said. "I have some work to do."

"Wait for me," Faulkner told him.

"If I wait," the bounty hunter said, "I'm going to have another drink."

"Okay," Faulkner said, "but no firewater. Just a beer."

"I'll see to it you're not charged," Gena told Tall Fellow.

"There you go," Tall Fellow said with a rare smile. "That's a good reason for me to wait."

Gena signaled to the bartender, who drew Tall Fellow another beer and set it down in front of him. Apparently, something in her signal meant there should be no charge. Faulkner wondered what kind of code this was that saloon owners had with bartenders.

"Shall we go?" she asked him.

"Lead the way."

In the office they took up their former positions, she behind the desk, and he seated across from her.

"Have you seen Blaine?" she asked.

"Seen and met."

"Really. Did he try to hire you?"

"He did," Faulkner said.

"To do what?"

"He didn't say yet," Faulkner said. "Just said he could use a man like me."

"Thinking about his offer?" she asked.

"That's what I told him," he said, "but I have another offer already."

She took a strongbox out from beneath her desk, set it on top and opened it.

"How much?" she asked.

He told her how much half would be. She flinched, but counted out the money and handed it across to him.

"Will that do it?"

"One more thing," he said.

"What's that?"

"One more dinner before I leave town."

She smiled and said, "I think that can be arranged."

CHAPTER 48

Jack Sunday didn't like leaving Gary Blaine to talk with Faulkner. They still had not settled the question of a partnership for him to kill the woman. Now if Blaine hired Faulkner, Sunday would be on the outside looking in. Suddenly, he wanted to be on the inside.

He was walking down the street toward his hotel when he saw Hobbs and a couple of the men coming toward him. When they spotted him they abruptly changed direction and crossed the street. Good, they were keeping to the agreement and staying away from him.

"I'm tellin' you," Hobbs said, as he and his *compadres* entered the Lucky Ace, "if somebody would just take care of Sunday we'd be a lot better off."

"Then who would plan the jobs?" one of the men asked him.

238

"And whose gang would it be?"

"Me," Hobbs said, "and mine."

"You?"

"What's the matter with me as leader?" Hobbs demanded angrily.

"Hobbs, the only way you're gonna get the others to accept you as leader is to kill Jack Sunday yerself. You man enough to do that?"

"Sure I am," Hobbs replied without thinking.

The other man grinned and said, "That I gotta see."

"Shut up," Hobbs said. "Let's get some beer."

When Faulkner came out of the office, Tall Fellow was still nursing his beer — if it was the same beer.

"Ask him," Tall Fellow said, pointing at the bartender. "Same one."

The barman nodded.

"You get paid?" Tall Fellow asked.

"Yup."

"Okay," Tall Fellow said. "Why don't you go and talk to those two bodyguards."

"What are you going to do?"

"I'm going to locate Jack Sunday."

"Don't try to take him."

"I know I can take him," Tall Fellow said,

"but I won't make a move until you're ready with your man."

"Okay," Faulkner said. "Suppose we meet back here in two hours. We should both have some useful information by then."

"Okay," Tall Fellow said. "Two hours. If one of us isn't here by then, he's in trouble."

"Don't," Faulkner said, "get into trouble."

"I never get into trouble on purpose," Tall Fellow pointed out.

"Just remember Denver."

"That was different!"

"I'm just saying . . ."

Faulkner walked over to the Lucky Ace and entered. He scanned the walls, saw the two openings that were large enough for a rifle barrel to poke out. He'd been in saloons in the old days when men armed with shotguns sat on a raised platform out in the open where everyone could see them. This was supposed to act as a deterrent, but it also gave the man the opportunity to act quickly in the event of trouble.

Blaine had his men hidden — at least, some of them. The two men who had drawn their guns on Faulkner and Tall Fellow were standing at the bar, talking with the bartender. Blaine himself was nowhere in sight. Faulkner remembered that Gena had told him Blaine had five bodyguards. He wondered if that included the bartender, or if he was still missing one.

He approached the two men at the bar. He noticed that while the saloon was full, the patrons gave the two bodyguards plenty of room.

"Here comes the Money Gun," one of them said.

"Money Gun," the other man said, chuckling. "We got the drop on 'im pretty good, didn't we?"

"We sure did."

"Your boss says you fellas will talk to me," Faulkner said, ignoring their jibes.

"About what?"

"About him," Faulkner said.

"Yeah, well, he said we could tell you some stuff."

"Which of you is Kirk, and which is Ben?" Faulkner asked. "Are you allowed to tell me that?"

"I'm Kirk," the tall, thin one said.

"I'm Ben."

"Bartender," Faulkner said, "I'll take a beer."

Kirk and Ben were already holding beer mugs.

"Comin' up," the man said. When he set the mug down he said, "Boss says it's on the house."

"Thanks."

"What's on yer mind?" Kirk asked.

"What kind of boss is Blaine?"

The two men exchanged a glance. The bartender ducked his head and walked away.

"That bad?"

"Look," Ben said, "our job is to keep him alive. We don't have to like the guy."

"Hey," Kirk said warningly.

"What the hell," Ben said. "If he offered this guy a job he deserves ta know."

"Also," Faulkner said, "if you scare me off I can't replace one of you."

"You ain't gonna replace one of us," Kirk said. "The boss needs you for . . . other things."

"Things that suit your . . . talents."

"He needs me to kill somebody?"

"He didn't tell you?" Kirk asked.

"Well, I haven't agreed to work for him yet."

"Better get the whole picture," Ben warned.

"And what would that be?"

The two men exchanged a glance, then looked around. There was no one within earshot.

"Come on," Faulkner said. "It's just us guys."

"Let's just say," Ben replied, "he's probably wonderin' if you've ever killed a woman."

CHAPTER 49

"He wants me to kill a woman?"

"Probably," Kirk said.

"He's been talkin' to Jack Sunday about doin' it," Ben said, "but the minute we heard who you were we knew he'd wanna talk to you."

"Do you know who the woman is?"

"Let's just say," Ben answered, "it's a competitor."

"We're getting off the trail here," Faulkner said, not surprised that if Gena wanted Blaine killed, he'd want her killed, too. "Does he pay well?"

Kirk snorted.

"If he does we don't get it."

"What about the way he treats you?"

"Like dirt," Ben said. "Like we're beneath him."

"And does he have others working for him?"

Kirk leaned in.

"He's real skittish abut gettin' killed," he said. "He's got five bodyguards."

"I see the rifle slots in the wall," Faulkner said.

"You got good eyes."

"What does he do when he goes out?"

"Takes two of us with him," Kirk said, "and the others are on the rooftops. He doesn't go anywhere at least two of us can't see him."

"So then I guess I wouldn't be one of his bodyguards," Faulkner said.

"Oh, no," Kirk said, "you'd be his pet killer."

"Almost sounds to me like you boys wouldn't be too upset if he got killed."

The two men leaned back against the bar.

"We ain't sayin' that," Kirk said.

"We ain't sayin' that at all," Ben said.

Suddenly, it was as if the two of them thought they'd said too much.

"Don't worry," Faulkner said, putting his beer mug down on the bar. "This is all just between us."

" 'Preciate that, Faulkner," Kirk said.

"We're sorry about razzin' ya," Ben said.

"No problem," Faulkner said. "Listen, do the other bodyguards feel the way you do?"

"Pretty much," Ben said.

"Then I guess there's no point in me talking to them. I'd get the same response."

"Probably," Ben said.

"So, you gonna take the job?" Kirk asked.

"I haven't decided yet," Faulkner said, "but you boys have given me something to think about."

As he turned to walk out, Kirk asked, "Hey, have you ever killed a woman?"

Faulkner didn't answer.

Tall Fellow went to the hotel he, Faulkner and Sunday were sharing. He knew what room Sunday was in, and crept down the hall to put his ear to the door. He thought he heard the man moving around in there, but couldn't be sure. He went back downstairs to the front desk, held out a dollar to the clerk.

"What's that fer?" He'd been dozing, and Tall Fellow thought the smell of the dollar had woken him up.

"The answer to a few questions."

"One dollar buys one question," the man said.

"Four bits per question," Tall Fellow countered.

The man thought a moment, then grabbed the dollar and said, "Yer on. You got two comin', so far."

■ ■ ■ ■

After Faulkner left the saloon, Ben and Kirk turned to lean on the bar. The bartender came over.

"You boys plan on goin' up against him?" he asked them.

"Hell, no," Kirk said. "For the money Blaine pays us, I ain't goin' up against a man with Faulkner's rep."

"Me, either," Ben said. "That man is a stone killer. You can see it in his eyes."

"So what are you gonna do if he is here for Blaine?" the barman asked.

"I don't know about you, Eddie," Ben said to the bartender, "but if he comes after Blaine I plan to get out of the way."

"Me, too," Kirk said, "and I recommend you do the same thing."

"What about Vin and Jimmy," the bartender said, "behind the false walls?"

"They can make up their own minds if and when the time comes," Kirk said.

"You boys don't have any desire to go after a man with a rep? Maybe get one of your own?"

"Go back to pouring drinks, Eddie," Kirk told the bartender. "You're startin' ta talk crazy."

CHAPTER 50

Faulkner didn't need two hours. He'd gotten what he needed. Five bodyguards or not, if Blaine had men working for him who didn't care if he lived or died, then he was vulnerable.

He'd noticed three other men in the saloon he recognized. Well, two, actually. They were the two he'd seen arguing at the poker table in the Ace the previous night. He assumed that the third man with them was also one of Sunday's men. It seemed pretty clear that while Sunday didn't want them around him, the men were sticking together. Less chance of someone throwing down on them that way. Maybe there had been more of the men in the saloon the night before.

If Jack Sunday's men were watching each other's backs, then nobody was watching his.

He was pretty sure Tall Fellow was going

to find out the same thing.

By the time Tall Fellow got back to the Happy Thief, Faulkner was already there. As he approached the bar Faulkner held a beer out to him.

"You expected me this early?"

"I think we both got what we wanted."

"You first," Tall Fellow said.

Faulkner told him what he had learned from the two Blaine bodyguards. He also told him he had seen three of Sunday's men in the Ace.

"I guess now we know why he said he needed to hire you," Tall Fellow said, "somebody he could count on."

"What about you?"

"Sunday's in his room. He splits his time between three or four places."

"His hotel, the restaurant across the street . . ." Faulkner started.

". . . the Lucky Ace, and one of the whorehouses," Tall Fellow finished.

"So all you've got to do," Faulkner said, "is stay away from the Ace, and catch him in one of the other three places."

"What about you?" Tall Fellow asked. "Can you wait until Blaine decides to leave his saloon?"

"I don't think so," Faulkner said. "I don't

want to be in Gunman's Crossing very much longer, now that some people know who I am. The word is bound to circulate."

"So what? You don't have any law in your background. Why will anyone care?"

"Somebody will want to make a try for my rep," Faulkner said. "It always happens. The sooner I get out of this town, the better."

"Then why not get out without doing the job?" the bounty hunter asked. "We'll take Sunday and leave."

"I already took the job," Faulkner said. "I already took half the money. There's no going back."

"Okay, then. What's the timing going to be?"

"I think I can convince Kirk and Ben to take a walk," Faulkner said. "Should take me about twenty minutes."

"I can keep Sunday in sight until then," Tall Fellow said. "Twenty minutes from when we leave here, right?"

"Better make it half an hour, just to be on the safe side."

"Okay," Tall Fellow said. "Thirty minutes."

Tall Fellow looked ready to leave.

"Before we go," Faulkner said, putting his

hand out to stop his friend, "tell me one thing."

"What's that?"

"This thing with Sunday — it's not about the bounty for you, is it?"

Tall Fellow hesitated, then said, "The money on Jack Sunday is big. It seems fitting to me that I bring him in, collect the money, and then try to do something about my eyes."

"I thought you said nothing could be done."

"There's a doctor in New York," Tall Fellow said. "He's real expensive. I heard that maybe he could do something."

"Why didn't you tell me this before?"

"I didn't want to appear foolish," Tall Fellow said. "Not in your eyes. You're the only man I respect, Faulkner."

"All right," Faulkner said. "Let's make damn sure you get Sunday, then."

"How do we do that?"

"We'll take him together."

"I take them alive if I can, Faulkner," Tall Fellow reminded him. "You take them dead."

"Your bounty," Faulkner said to his friend, "your call."

CHAPTER 51

Gary Blaine thought that all his problems were solved. He'd made a grave error in approaching Jack Sunday, but Faulkner was going to help him correct it. First, the hired gun was going to get rid of Gena Miller for him. She'd been a thorn in his side since her husband had been killed. Privately, Blaine suspected that Gena herself had shot Thornton Miller in the back. That alone made her much more dangerous than anyone had ever thought.

Then, after he got rid of Gena, Faulkner would take care of Jack Sunday. Killing the man was the only way to get out from under his demands of a partnership. Blaine didn't know who the man thought he was, but he was certainly not going to be a partner, even in the most minor sense. No, all that Jack Sunday was going to get for his trouble was . . . death.

Faulkner would see to that.

Faulkner would be the first man in Blaine's employ that he could really count on. Little by little he'd get rid of the other idiots. He was sure he could convert Faulkner from a top-notch money gun into a first-rate bodyguard.

All it would take was money.

Gena Miller thought that all her problems were solved. Of course, the only problem she had was Gary Blaine. Not only was he her main competitor — plus the little fact that he wanted her dead — but she knew he suspected that she had killed Thornton. If she were a man she would have bragged that she'd killed the great Thornton Miller. But she was a woman, and she didn't want anyone to know about it. There was no macho in her killing of her husband, just a desire to get rid of an abusive man.

She'd gotten rid of one man in her life herself. It would take Faulkner to get rid of the other one.

Tall Fellow could see in Faulkner's eyes that the man did not think him foolish, nor did he pity him. All he saw was friendship, and he was willing to accept that from Faulkner.

His eyes were his problem, and he'd try to get them taken care of on his own. But he didn't mind accepting Faulkner's help with Jack Sunday.

"Indian," Faulkner said, as they left the Happy Thief, "the only way this is going to work is to put him down. For good."

"I thought you said it was my call," Tall Fellow said, stopping right outside the batwing doors. "Wasn't that you a minute ago? 'Your bounty, your call?' Remember that?"

"I do remember it, and I said it," Faulkner replied. "But I've been thinking it over. We put Sunday down, then go right to the Lucky Ace and take care of Blaine."

"I have one problem with this," Tall Fellow said.

"What's that?"

"I'm your friend and I'll back your play," Tall Fellow said, "but I won't kill a man in cold blood. That's your profession, and I don't judge you for it. Maybe I did back in the beginning, but not anymore. We've been through too much together for me to judge you."

"I appreciate that, and I'll accept whatever form your help comes in."

"Then we can proceed."

They stepped down off the boardwalk and crossed the street.

■ ■ ■ ■

Sunday left the hotel and headed for the whorehouse owned by Gary Blaine. He needed to release some of his tension and anger before he talked to Blaine again. If the man was trying to edge him out already — before they'd even come to an agreement — he was going to be sorry. But Sunday needed to be coolheaded and calm when he confronted the man.

That meant a big blonde with wide hips and gigantic tits was going to get the ride of her life.

When Faulkner and Tall Fellow reached the hotel, the bounty hunter said to the money gun, "Give the man a dollar."

"What for?"

"Because I don't have any left."

"No, what's the dollar for?"

"Oh, that's so he'll answer some questions."

Faulkner looked at the clerk, the same man who had checked him in.

"Oh," Faulkner said, "I think he'll answer some questions without getting paid, won't you, friend?"

Chapter 52

Before going into his saloon — which was close to packed at the moment — Blaine checked on the men behind the false walls.

He asked each of them, "Do you know what Jack Sunday looks like?"

They answered in turn, yes.

"You better damn know him on sight, you sonofabitch," Blaine said to each man. "And keep him in your sights if he walks into my place. You got it?"

They both said they did.

"If anything goes wrong I'll have your hides."

They nodded.

"And did you see the man I was sitting with today?" he asked, as an afterthought.

They said they did.

"His name is Faulkner. Yeah, I can see you've heard of him. Keep him in your sights, too, if he comes in. I don't want to take any chances."

They said they would. Then, as Blaine walked away, they each wondered what he'd look like with a bullet in his back.

"See?" Faulkner said. "I told you he'd answer questions without getting paid."

"I had an arrangement with him," Tall Fellow said. "Four bits a question."

"I saved you money through a little intimidation," Faulkner said.

"I don't like scaring people."

"Tall Fellow, you're half Indian," Faulkner told him. "You automatically scare people."

They walked to the end of town where Blaine had his whorehouse situated. Sunday was not at his hotel, not in the restaurant and not at the saloon. This was the only other place he could be — unless he had suddenly broken his pattern.

"This remind you of anything?" Faulkner asked.

"Yeah," Tall Fellow said. "Buckland."

"If that other fella hadn't come out of the room across the hall, and assumed we were law, we would have had Buckland easy."

"Figures Sunday would like whorehouses," Tall Fellow said. "He learned from Buckland."

Sunday was giving the whore a thorough

going-over. When he was finished with her, she'd never be the same. She was a big girl, though, and she was giving as good as she got. Sunday remembered Buckland used to do this with smaller women, but he didn't like small women. When he smacked a woman he liked to feel meat, and it was the same when he fucked one. And when he was doing both at the same time, it was doubly important.

The gal yelped and yowled whether he hit her or porked her. He had the feeling she liked both just fine.

Hobbs walked over to where the two body-guards were standing at the bar.

"Afternoon, Kirk."

"Hobbs. This is Ben. Hobbs came in with the Sunday gang."

"Sunday?" Ben asked. "I never see you with him. He's always here alone."

"That's how he wants it," Hobbs said. "Can't associate with the likes of us."

"Hmm," Ben said.

"What?" Kirk asked.

"Maybe Hobbs here should tell his boss about the money gun."

"What's this?"

"Fella named Faulkner rode into town yesterday."

"I know that name," Hobbs said.

"Well," Ben said, "he don't usually come into a town to say howdy. He's usually after somebody."

"And you think he may be after Sunday?" Hobbs asked.

"Well," Ben sad, "he did ride in real soon after you fellas did. Might want to warn your boss about it."

"Right now my boss is probably beatin' the shit out of a whore," Hobbs said. "And remember I said he don't wanna associate with us? Well, he likes it even less when he's interrupted while he's tearin' up some whore."

"I hope he ain't tearin' up Becky," Kirk said. "I like Becky."

"That fat-assed blonde?" Ben asked.

"She's got a fine ass," Kirk said.

And he, Ben and Hobbs started talking about all the women they'd known with fine asses on them.

Faulkner and Tall Fellow entered the whore-house to be greeted by the madam, a busty woman in her fifties with pasty skin.

"This the whorehouse owned by Gary Blaine?" Faulkner asked.

"It is," she said, then added, "don't tell

me he sent you fellas over for a free poke, too?"

"No, ma'am," Faulkner said. "We're not interested in a poke right now."

"That's a bold-faced lie," she said. "Men are always interested in a poke. It's all they think about."

"Okay," Faulkner said, "let me rephrase it. While we're interested, and we have the wherewithal, we just don't have the time."

"Oh," she said. "Then what —"

"He sent someone else over for a free one?" Tall Fellow asked.

"He did."

"Where is he now?"

"In the room all that yellin' and cryin' is comin' from."

Faulkner looked at Tall Fellow.

"Inside or out?"

"I'll take the inside."

"Good luck," Faulkner said, and hurried outside.

CHAPTER 53

Tall Fellow went up the stairs and followed the sound of the woman's voice to a room. Having learned from previous experience, he opened the door to the room right across the hall. A tall, gangly young man was putting it to a Chinese whore from behind, and they both stopped to stare at him.

"Sorry," Tall Fellow said. "Just wanted to tell you not to come running out of this room no matter what you hear."

"Mister," the boy said, "I ain't about to take my dick outta this here whore until I'm done."

Tall Fellow looked at the woman. She was small and fragile-looking, with slanted eyes and very black hair that was a mess from having been pulled.

"Good lad," he said, and closed the door.

Outside, Faulkner worked his way around to the back of the building. Above him he could see a row of windows. He hoped Sunday was in one of those rooms. If he was in a room across the hall, with no window, Tall Fellow was on his own.

He settled down to wait.

Tall Fellow moved to the door, drew his gun and then kicked the door open. The sight of a big naked butt greeted him, pale except for the redness on each cheek from somebody slapping there.

Sunday was also naked, but he didn't hesitate. As soon as the door crashed open he went for his gun, hanging on the bedpost. The girl screamed, got up to her knees, and ended up right between Tall Fellow and Sunday.

Tall Fellow hesitated.

Sunday didn't.

One shot.

Faulkner heard the single shot, was tempted to run back into the building, but he stood his ground and was rewarded for it. A half-dressed Jack Sunday appeared in the window, then dropped down to the ground. He landed like a cat, pants and gun belt in one hand and gun in the other.

"You're quick, Jack," Faulkner said. "But not quick enough."

Sunday stared at Faulkner with hatred.

"This how you're gonna take my partnership from me?" he asked.

"Partnership?"

"Me and Blaine was gonna be partners, until you showed up."

"This has got nothing to do with a partnership," Faulkner said. "There's a price on your head, and we tracked you here to get it."

"A bounty hunter? I never heard you were a bounty hunter, Faulkner."

"I helping a friend who, by the way, better be alive up there."

"Stupid whore got in the way," Sunday said. "She caught the bullet. Your man is all right and should be down here any minute, so I got no time to waste. Don't suppose you'd give me a fair chance?"

"Not what I'm about, Jack."

"Too bad."

"Don't —" Faulkner said, but it was too late. The man was grabbing for his gun. Faulkner fired once, put Jack Sunday down for good with the single shot.

Tall Fellow came running from the alley and stopped when he saw Sunday on the ground.

"He gave me no choice, Indian," Faulkner sad.

"I believe you," Tall Fellow said. "Dead money spends just as well as live money."

"Think anyone heard those shots?"

"Just two? Spaced out like that? Even if somebody did they don't care, as long as nobody's shooting at them."

"We need to move fast," Faulkner said. "What do we do with him?"

Tall Fellow spotted a bunch of crates and said, "Let's put him behind there for now. He'll keep until we get back."

They lifted the dead outlaw and dumped him behind the crates, then tossed his pants and gun belt after him. Faulkner picked up the dead man's gun and tucked it into his belt.

"Just in case," he said. "Now let's get over to the Lucky Ace."

CHAPTER 54

They walked through town toward the Lucky Ace. Nobody was on the street in Gunman's Crossing.

"You know," Faulkner said to Tall Fellow, "this business of having no law around might not be too bad. This town is actually pretty quiet."

"I know," Tall Fellow said. "I expected more shootouts in the streets."

When they reached the Lucky Ace they paused. Briefly, Faulkner described to Tall Fellow where the slots for the guns were.

"My guess is the walls are false, and probably thin. Don't be afraid to shoot through them."

"Got it."

"You take the one on the right," he continued. "I'll take the left."

"Right, I've got the right."

"And watch the bartender," Faulkner said. "He's got a gun under the bar."

"Don't they all?"

"He might be the fifth bodyguard."

"I got that, too."

"I'll do the talking."

"Be my guest."

Together, they walked through the batwing doors.

Blaine saw Faulkner enter with Tall Fellow, whom he didn't know.

Kirk and Ben saw them enter, knowing both men instantly.

The bartender saw them, moved to stand in front of his gun.

The two men behind the false walls saw Faulkner and raised their rifles. They didn't have time to do much else.

Faulkner drew his gun and the extra gun, while Tall Fellow produced his. They both shots holes in the walls while patrons in the place sat stunned.

"This is private business," Faulkner shouted. "Anybody interested in taking a hand?"

Men exchanged glances, but nobody was even willing to stand up. This was an interruption in their evening they hoped would not last long.

Faulkner looked at Kirk and Ben.

"Go for your guns or take a walk."

"We're walkin'," Kirk said without hesitation. He walked and Ben walked right out the door behind him.

Faulkner looked at the bartender.

"Pull that hogleg or get away from it."

The bartender hesitated, then backed away, showing his hands.

Faulkner looked over at the three of Jack Sunday's men. They were all watching the action with interest.

"You boys should know that Jack Sunday is dead," Faulkner said. "We're claiming the bounty on his head."

The three men stared at Faulkner, and then one man stood up, showing his hands.

"That suits us, Mister," Hobbs said. "We was lookin' for a new leader, anyway."

"You better get moving, then," Faulkner said.

"Yes, sir," Hobbs waved at the other two men, "we're movin'. We're gonna gather up the rest of the gang and head out."

"That's a good idea," Faulkner said. "Anybody still in town after we're finished here is fair game."

Faulkner looked over at Gary Blaine, who was standing at his table, watching them.

"What's going on, Faulkner?" Blaine demanded. "What the hell?"

"I'm turning down your offer of employment, Blaine," Faulkner said.

"You're dead," Blaine said. "You hear me, Faulkner? Dead."

"No," Faulkner said, "I'm afraid you are."

He shot him once.

CHAPTER 55

Early the next morning Faulkner met Tall Fellow at the livery stable. The bounty hunter had already tied Jack Sunday to the back of his horse. The rest of Sunday's men had left town as quickly as Hobbs had been able to collect them.

Faulkner had collected the rest of his money from Gena Miller over supper. She'd offered him more, but he didn't want to get tangled up with a woman who would kill her own husband. You just couldn't trust a woman who would do that.

"You ready to go?" Tall Fellow asked.

"As soon as I saddle up."

Nobody in town had made a fuss over them killing Jack Sunday and Gary Blaine, or the two bodyguards who had been behind the walls. There really was a mind-your-own-business policy in Gunman's Crossing that worked to their definite advantage.

Tall Fellow waited outside the livery for

Faulkner, who eventually saddled his horse and walked it out.

"Where you headed, Faulkner?" Tall Fellow asked.

"With you," Faulkner said.

"I've just got to get to a town with some law, a telegraph and a bank, and I can collect my money."

"You gonna have enough for that doctor in New York?" Faulkner asked.

Tall Fellow shrugged.

"Who knows? If not, I'll just have to track down a few more bounties."

"Maybe not." Faulkner held out an envelope.

"What's that?"

"The money I got paid for killing Blaine," Faulkner said. "I charged her double."

"That's your money."

"I'm throwing it in with yours, Indian," Faulkner said to his friend. "And if you don't mind, I'll just go along with you to New York to see that doctor."

Tall Fellow looked at him.

"I don't know what to say."

"Just take the money, bounty hunter."

Tall Fellow took the envelope.

"You're footing the expenses, though," Faulkner told him.

Tall Fellow grinned and said, "I wouldn't have it any other way, Money Gun. Thanks."

The employees of Thorndike Press hope you have enjoyed this Large Print book. All our Thorndike and Wheeler Large Print titles are designed for easy reading, and all our books are made to last. Other Thorndike Press Large Print books are available at your library, through selected bookstores, or directly from us.

For information about titles, please call:
(800) 223-1244

or visit our Web site at:
http://gale.cengage.com/thorndike

To share your comments, please write:
Publisher
Thorndike Press
295 Kennedy Memorial Drive
Waterville, ME 04901